AF574291

HEADS AND TALES

Written by Cully Gage
Illustrated by Susan Van Riper Krill
Cover Photo by Hoyt Avery

Library of Congress Card No. 82-72359
ISBN 0-932212-28-X
First Edition - June 1982
Published by Avery Color Studios
AuTrain, Michigan 49806

CONTENTS

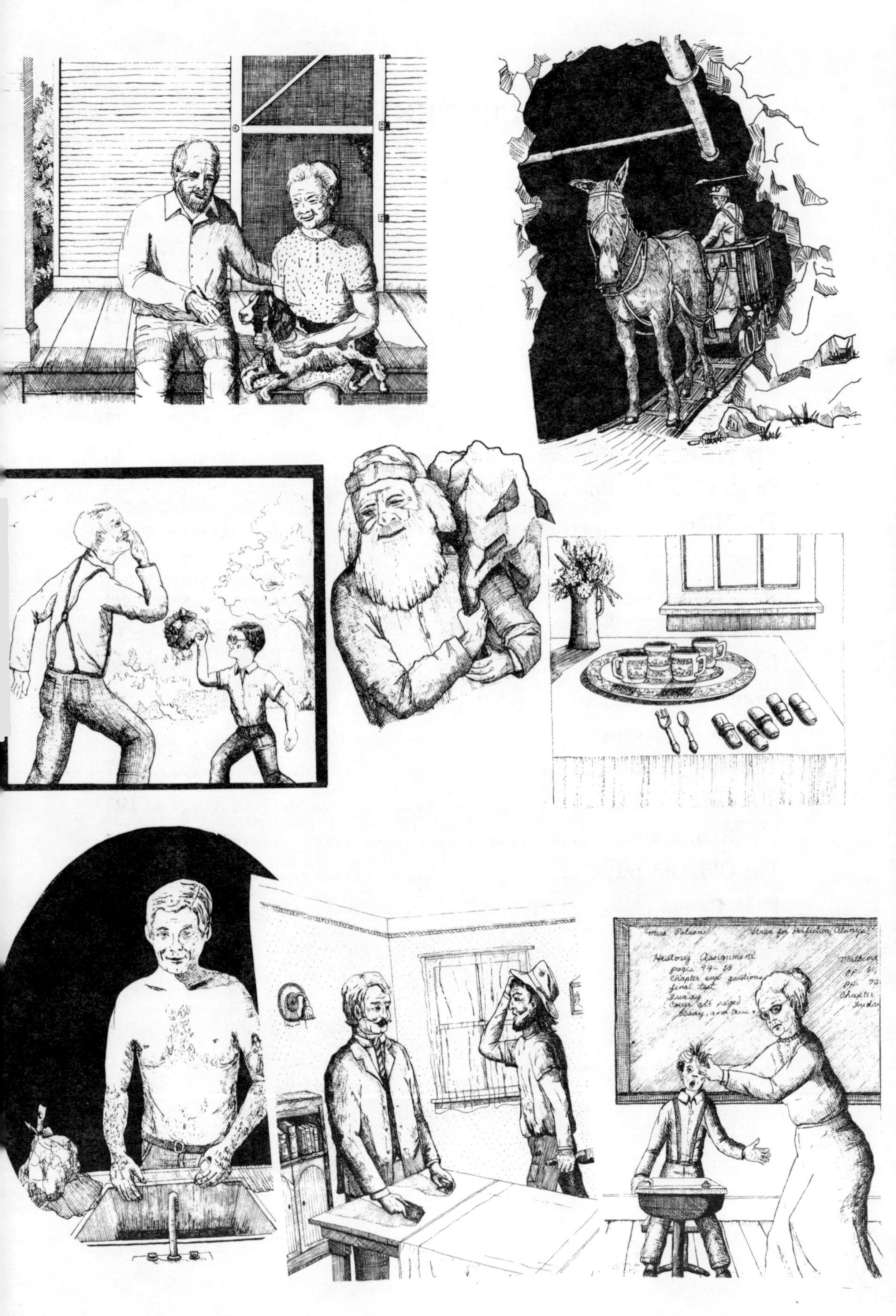
Strive for Perfection Always!
History Assignment
pages 44-
Chapter end questions
final test
Friday
Cover all pages

FOREWORD

I always thought that I began writing these stories about the people I knew when I was a boy in the forest village of Tioga so that my grandchildren could know how we lived at the beginning of this century. Now, I'm not so sure. With a white beard and now almost eighty years old, I suspect that my motive was merely self indulgence. I simply wanted to remember those fascinating characters again. Certainly I had no premonition that I could ever write two books, let alone three of them, about the old days in the Upper Peninsula of Michigan, but here, God help me, is the third. If there is dotage in my ancedotage, I shall not be surprised.

Yet I feel too that these tales of how we coped with hard times in the past may have some meaningfulness today. Without any Social Security or A.D.C., or any other help, we survived and lived a good life because we knew each other and cared for each other. Though the great white pines were gone, and the mines kept petering out, we still coped and had fun doing it.

Many who have read these Northwoods Readers have asked me if the tales are true. All I can say is that they are true to the life we led way back then. If there is laughter in these pages, there was laughter in our lives, and that was what helped us make it through the winter.

Cully Gage

GYPSIES

"The gypsies are coming! The gypsies are in town! Lock your doors! Hide under the bed!" Every August that cry ran up our hill street long before they appeared in their covered wagons in route to their usual camping grounds beyond our long closed mine. Little shivers of delight and fear beset me as I watched the little procession. First came a man with gold rings in his ears, swarthy as an Indian, leading the way with long steps. Then came the covered wagon hauled by one horse with a boy holding the reins. Inside the wagon we could see people, in colorful clothes, behind the puckered opening and sometimes we heard them talking or singing. Tied to the rear of the wagon was a string of horses, three or four of them, some carrying packs. Most years there were two or three of these gypsy wagons but this particular August there was only one. Perhaps others would be joining them later.

My father scoffed at the belief that all gypsies were thieves or that they kidnapped little children. In other years he'd treated some of them up at their encampment for various hurts or illnesses and never charged them anything for his services. "They're poor folk living by their wits," my father said. "They're wanderers by nature and there've been times I've envied them. No moss on those rolling stones. They're free. I like 'em!" One of Dad's favorite possessions was a big yellow calabash pipe some gypsies had given him.

The gypsies spent about a week working over our village. The man was a tinker and scissors grinder, and since these services were in much demand, he was given work at some of our houses even though we wouldn't ever let him come inside. My mother, who had a leaky tea kettle, a pan whose handle had come off, and a big copper washboiler with a hole in it, let me watch the gypsy man repair them. After sanding around the holes, he'd light a little alcohol lamp and blow a jet of flame at the spot till it was hot enough. Then from his pack, he got out a soldering iron, heated it too, put it in some kind of paste and quick as a wink, the thing was fixed. He knew his stuff all right, but he didn't say a word to me or smile. When he was done, he motioned to me to get my mother who thanked him and asked him the price. In answering, I noticed that he had a thick, odd accent but we gathered that he would settle for two pounds of sugar, a peck of potatoes and twenty-five cents. She gave them to him and he went on to the next house.

That afternoon, two gypsy women in colorful dresses with huge sleeves came to our back door. They also had gold rings in their ears, and wore gold necklaces and bracelets. Their English was even harder to understand but they were selling ecru lace and silk scarves of very bright colors. The gypsies wore these scarves around their heads, layer upon layer, and it was sure pretty to see them laid out on the green grass beside our back step. Mother bought some lace and an orange scarf but had trouble when they kept wanting to haggle and insisting on more money. Finally she put down a five dollar bill and indicated that was all she would pay. They jabbered some more, then took it, but they also snatched up the orange scarf before they left. Mother felt cheated but was glad to get rid of them.

I suspect the gypsies got a more hostile reception at most of the other houses on our street than they did at ours. They had a bad name for stealing and cheating and they were slick at it. People claimed they could steal the shoes off your feet and your socks would never know it. And speaking of socks, that was why M. C. Flinn, when he heard the gypsies were in town, hired Charley Olafson to be at the door of the store to turn them away if they tried to enter. He had good reason. The year before some gypsy women had put up a commotion back of the grocery counter and then, after they left, M. C. had found that their kids had swiped three pair of men's work socks. Mr. Flinn knew they had because he'd put out six pairs that very morning and no one else had bought any. Of course, he charged them twice as much for the dried apples they'd boughten but M.C. Flinn didn't like to get taken. Anyway, Charley turned them away when this bunch tried to come in.

Somehow the gypsies fascinated me and so one evening when they were still camping up at the mine, I tried to get Mullu to go up there with me to hide in the bushes and see what they were doing. He was scared but came along and we watched them eating their supper meal. There were six of them altogether sitting around their fire, eating something from a big black kettle hung over it. They'd take their bowls and dip out some stew or goulash or something, then break off a chunk of bread to dip in it.No forks or knives. Not even spoons. Sometimes they'd tip the bowls up to their faces to get the last of it. We'd heard that gypsies would play the fiddle and dance but we didn't see any of that -- just people eating and jabbering together. Mullu and I left feeling disappointed.

Gypsies were known far and wide for being smart horse traders and you had to be pretty careful or they'd skin you good. In our town we had two men who fancied themselves as being pretty slick traders, not just of horses and mules, but for almost anything. Their names were Pete Hummel and Herb Anderson. I've always had a hard time remembering Herb's real name because everyone called him the "Deacon." Not that he went to church much, if he ever went at all, but he sure looked and acted like a deacon, pious as hell. They say he was swapping things even when he was a kid - pencils for jacknives, jacknives for a batch of marbles, and so on until he came up with a pig and a heifer even before he quit school. Just a natural trader, the Deacon was. He'd swap anything for anything. They told a tale about him that once a fellow over by Michigamme so much admired a feisty white mare the Deacon had, he said he'd give his wife for that horse. The Deacon didn't bat an eye. "All right," he says, "how much to boot?" That probably was just talk but the Deacon had done right well by his trading. Had a barn and barnyard full of stuff he'd traded for - an old mule, pigs and chickens, horse collars, a cutter, oh there were piles of things.

The other trader, Pete Hummel, mainly specialized in horses, cows and mules. He knew a lot about them and the tricks that people used to skin you, when swapping. That's why the Deacon asked Pete to come along with him when he went up to the gypsy camp. As they rode up there in the buggy behind his old horse, the Deacon explained. "I seen them going up the street when they come in," he said. "And they was leading three horses behind the wagon. Two of the horses were dogs not worth a handful of oats but there was one big brown one that looked pretty good. Maybe worth trading for. I figure they got too many people to be in that one wagon and I got an old buckboard to home they might be a-needing."

"You mean that one with the broken spring that you painted over, the one with the wobbly wheel?" asked Pete. "Yah, I know it. But if that horse is as good as you say he looks, you ain't going to get no Gypsy to go for it. What you going to throw in for boot, Deacon?"

"Oh, I dunno," answered the Deacon. "Best wait and see what's up there. I been skinned before by gypsies. Once long ago I traded a good heifer for a mule they had and come to find out it was a moonie - went nigh blind ever so often, specially in the dark of the moon. You know the tricks, Pete, better'n I do, so if I trade for that horse, you look it over good for me."

"Aw, hell, Deacon," Peter replied. "You know the tricks pretty good yourself. I see you've sheared and trimmed old Betsey's mane and pumped air in the hollows above her eyes and colored the gray hairs with permanganate potash soaked in coffee. Thought you had a new horse when you first drove up. I bet you filed her teeth too."

The Deacon grinned and nodded. "Yup! Old Betsey's got the teeth of a seven year old now." he said. "Not bad for a fifteen year old mare."

When they got near the mine the Deacon touched up the horse with his whip and they trotted briskly into the campground. The two men got out of the buggy and went over to the gypsy man who was sitting on a stump by the grazing horses.

After the usual preliminaries of looking at all of the other horses and explaining that he could use a spare horse but didn't really need one, the Deacon asked if he could look over the big brown one if it was for trade. The gypsy nodded and the two men sure gave it a going over. They looked in its mouth and found that the teeth were sound with good crowns and hadn't been filed. Probably five years old or less. The hollows above the eyes were firm. They fanned a hand past the eyes and it blinked so it wasn't blind. They went over the body for knots and spavins but found none. They lifted both hind hooves to see if it was a kicker or if there was anything wrong with the frogs but there wasn't and it had a fairly new pair of shoes. Pete even smelled its breath to make sure it hadn't been given a spoonful of dynamite with its feed. No, no acrid odor. It had good hearing. It was alert. Good front legs, too.

Pete took the Deacon aside. "Gawdamighty!" he said. "That's the best horse I seen for years. Nothing wrong with him but you'd better know if he can stand hitching. Ask to take him out for a little ride."

The Deacon nodded. "Might still be a kicker bad enough to stove in the buggy or break the cross tree," he said. "And maybe he's a heaver though I don't see the sign. Or maybe he'll go lame. That damned horse is too good to be true.

With the gypsy's permission, they hitched it to the buggy and drove to Flinn's store and back. The big brown had a fine gait and responded to the reins and whip as a good horse should. They stopped at the store to see if it would stay put or start creeping. No! That horse would stand without hitching. They trotted back swiftly and the horse wasn't even breathing hard when they unhitched it.

"Damn my bones, Deacon," Pete said. "If you can get that horse, you sure better. Never seen a better one. For ten cents I'd start trading for it myself."

Then the haggling began and it lasted two or three hours before they made a deal. The Deacon would trade his horse for the brown one and throw in a buckboard, three sacks of oats, and give twenty five dollars to boot. He'd be back next morning bringing the buckboard and oats. If the gypsy man didn't want the buckboard, he could have the buggy. That was the swap.

All that night the Deacon worried about the trade. There must be something wrong. That horse was just too good,but scratch his brain, he wasn't able to think of a thing that might mean he was getting skinned. Except dealing with a Gypsy horse trader. Of course, the gypsy was getting a pretty fair deal, too. He'd have a good old sound horse and a buckboard to relieve the crowding of six people in that old covered wagon. That made sense. Nevertheless...Finally he got to sleep.

The next morning the Deacon, after rubbing old Betsey's coat with oil to make it gleam, hitched her up to the buggy, tied the buckboard on behind it and made his way to the campground. As he approached it he was relieved to see the big brown horse still there. The thought had come to him that maybe Pete had beaten him to it. And he was relieved again when the gypsy took the buckboard with the broken spring and the wobbly wheel instead of his buggy. He said goodbye to old Betsey, hitched the brown horse to his buggy and sped down the street to his home. A pleasure to drive. The Deacon could hardly believe his good fortune.

But that afternoon everything fell apart. He had fed the brown horse well and currycombed and brushed him until its hide glistened. An easy horse to put the bridle on, too. Some horses fought the bridle but not this one. The Deacon drove to Flinn's store and then decided to return by the back road to Lake Tioga. Gad, that was a good horse. A keeper. No trading him.

But on the way back when they came to the first little hill, the horse balked! Just planted all four feet solidly on the ground and wouldn't move. The Deacon whipped him and pleaded with him. He tried to lead him by the bridle. No! The brown horse, damn him, wouldn't budge. "Oh God," prayed the Deacon. "I've got a real genuine ten carat balker, I have. What the devil will I do now?"

There wasn't anything to do except wait and hope to hell that the horse would start going again. The Deacon knew that you could beat a balky horse with a two by four until he'd roll his eyes back so you could see the white of them but it wouldn't move until it got good and ready. It took the Deacon three hours to get back from Lake Tioga - just a mile. Odd thing was, the horse would trot on level ground, but give it a little hill and he'd stop and you couldn't move him if you'd build a fire under him. There was no cure for a real bad balking horse. He'd been skinned by gypsies again.

Luckily no one had seen the brown horse balking so the Deacon figured on trading him as fast as he could, and he thought, of course, of Pete Hummel. Twasn't a nice thing to do but in trading, as in love, all is fair. Caveat Emptor! Let the trader beware. After all, Pete had looked the brown horse over and had said it was a good trade. Maybe it was his turn to be skinned.

So, for about a week, the Deacon made a point of driving over to Pete's house or past it every day with the new horse because fortunately it was all on the level. He sure didn't try to go up our hill street. Then, toward the end of that time, he stopped to dicker with Pete about trading for Pete's buckboard. Not trading the horse, mind you, but maybe Pete would trade his buckboard, which was almost new, for that heifer the Deacon had in his barnyard. No, Pete wasn't interested in the heifer, nor in the cutter, nor in anything else. But maybe, he said, if the Deacon would consider trading the brown horse they could dicker. He'd been mighty impressed with that horse.

The Deacon said he wasn't interested. He'd never had a horse so easy to handle or so easy to drive. While, as a trader, he'd never say no to any deal if it were good enough, he felt he had the horse he always wanted. So it went day after day with Pete Hummel grudgingly raising the offer. Finally, the Deacon gave in when Pete said he'd trade his own horse and his new buckboard and throw in fifty dollars to boot. Pete's horse wasn't much better than old Betsey had been but she was a lot younger so the Deacon felt he'd got the best of the trade. At least he'd got rid of that balker. He gloated a little.

That was why he was a bit surprised when a couple of weeks later Pete Hummel drove up with the brown horse and suggested they take a little ride to Lake Tioga and back. Pete didn't seem to be at all upset over having been taken either. "Never had such a fine horse," he said. He thanked the Deacon for trading with him.

Off they trotted down to the lake and then, on the way back, when they came to the little hill where Brownie had first balked, the horse began to slow down a bit and the Deacon knew it was about to balk just as it had done with him there. But Pete merely tickled the brown horse's tail with his whip, didn't really strike it at all, and the horse lunged forward. That same thing happened two more times and then finally Brownie really did balk. Stopped right there and rolled back its eyes. The Deacon couldn't help grinning a bit even though he knew it'd be a long time before they got home. He waited for Pete to start cursing both him and the horse.

But Pete didn't. He got out of the buggy and went over to the horse, touched it on the tail with his whip and then whispered something in its ear. Brownie took off in a hurry and Pete had to run to jump back in the buggy.

"I don't have him quite broke from that little balking habit yet," he explained. "But he's coming fine. Give me another week and he'll never balk again." The brown horse didn't balk once all the rest of the way home.

The Deacon was sure mystified and a bit upset. Nobody could break a real balking horse of the habit. What was it Pete had whispered in his ear? Unable to stand it, he finally asked him.

"I say the secret words," Pete replied. "Learned 'em from my pappy. They always work on a balky horse and all you got to do is tickle him with a whip just before you say 'em. Then after that you don't even have to talk to him. Just use the tickle. That's all you need, once he's trained."

Well, the whole business sure mortified the Deacon and he kept puzzling over those secret words of Pete's. They'd sure be handy. The Deacon knew other people had balky horses he might trade for. Could make a real profit knowing how to cure a balky horse. And it sure garred him to see Pete trotting that fine horse up our hill street day after day. Finally, he couldn't bear it another moment.

"Pete," he said. "Tell me what you said to that horse and I'll pay you five dollars."

"Nope," said Pete. "Won't tell you them secret words until you give me back my boot - fifty dollars."

It took some weeks of brooding before the Deacon finally gave in and handed over the money.

“I say, ‘Screw the Deacon!’ three times and blow in his ear,” Pete said with a grin. “It’s the blowing that does it. A horse can’t stand that. Balk or no balk, you blow in his ear and he’s got to get up and go. My pappy taught me.”

THE HAUNTED WHOREHOUSE

As Mullu and I emerged at dusk from Hatsnatcher Swamp, having followed the old river trail along the Tioga, we saw a speck of firelight by the big slough. We'd had a long day trout fishing and were both very wet and cold. There had been places along the river bank where the alders were so tangled it was easier to wade in the water even if you had to go in up to your armpits and put your worm can under your hat. Yes, we were cold, it being early in September when more sensible fishermen had long quit the streams. Mullu and I had hoped to catch a few of the big spawner brook trout that often showed up at the first hint of frost but all we'd caught were a few little ones. Wet butt and no fish again. A fire would sure feel good.

When we reached the fire we found Dick Duggan, a very old former miner, tending his trot line for bullhead. A black coffee pail hung from a bar between two forked sticks and it boiled over just as we got there. "Want some coffee, boys? You ain't got no whiskers to strain the grounds but she'll hot you up all the way down yer gizzard." The old man poured some coffee into a dirty soup can that had seen better days.

"No thanks, Dick. Just want to warm ourselves before setting out for home. Had any luck yet? We almost got skunked." Mullu's voice shivered as much as his knees as he turned his back to the flames.

The old man was glad of the company. "Ah, yer crazy going for trout so late in the season." he said. "Even if you get a few, they'll be slimy at best. It's bullhead time, boys, bullhead time. You can't catch a better eatin' fish than a fall bullhead, no siree."

Just then a cowbell clattered. "That makes three of 'em I've got on the line," the old man said. "Better bait up again." Hand over hand, he hauled up the clothesline and laid it in loops on the bank as three bullheads kicked around on the ground. We were interested because although we'd done a lot of fishing, we'd never used a trot line. Dick had strung about eight droplines from his clothesline, each with a worm covered hook, and at the end of the clothesline were two heavy horseshoes. After rebaiting, Dick grabbed a length of clothesline, whirled the horseshoes around his head and then let them fly way out into the slough. He then propped up and tightened the line with a big forked stick, reattached the cowbell and poured himself another can of coffee.

"That's pretty slick," I said. "I've only caught one bullhead in my life and the bugger horned me when I took it off the hook. My hand was sore for over a week and I never did clean or eat the fish. How do you clean a bullhead without getting hurt, Dick?"

"Nuthin' to it, boy. Nuthin' to it. I take the hook out with pliers like you see and when I get home I nail the head to my barn door. Then you cut 'em around the gills and they skin out right easy. Nuthin' to it."

"Are they really good eating?" Mullu asked, looking at the ugly fish squirming in the pail.

"Are they good eatin'? They the best. No bones. All white meat. You got to fry 'em crisp, though. Crisp brown." Dick smacked his lips. "I be feeding good tonight," he said.

The old man saw that we were getting ready to go and wanted to hold us a little longer. "Bullheads is good for more than eating," he said. "They keep haunts away, too" he said.

"Aw, I don't believe in ghosts," said Mullu. "There aren't any."

"The hell they ain't. I tell you I know. Maybe you can't always see 'em but they there."

"How do bullheads keep ghosts away, Dick?" I asked.

"Why you nail one on top each door of the house. Haunts, they won't pass a bullhead door. You boys got a lot of larning to do yet, saying there no haunts." The old man was indignant. "I seen 'em and heerd 'em and feeled 'em. I know. Tell you what you do. You go down to the old haunted whorehouse back of the depot and hang around some night and you'll hear one a-yelling. Though she be dead and buried long ago, her haunt can't leave the place."

"What's the story, Dick?" I asked. "I never heard of any whorehouse in town."

"Ah, I s'pose it was afore yer time. Yeah, afore you boys were born even. Maybe twenty, thirty year ago, when they were still driving pine logs down this river. Every spring, a madam and her whores come up on the train from Green Bay to take care of them lumberjacks coming out of the camps, horney as hell and hungry for she-meat. Well, that madam and her girls would bed 'em down in that old house till their wages was all gone. Oh, they'd screw some of the farmers and iron miners too as a sideline, but it was the lumberjacks and rivermen as was the best pickings. Then when they'd cleaned up plenty, the whores would go back to Green Bay to wait for next spring. You boys never hear about that? Everybody know that whorehouse."

"No," I said. "That's news to me. Where is the old whorehouse and how come you know it's haunted?"

"It's the last house on the road out to the slaughter house," Dick replied. "The one that's all boarded up with a big hole in the foundation. You've probably gone by it. On the railroad side of the road."

I nodded and the old man continued. "Here's how it come to have haunts. I was a-working for Henry Thompson then. He was the mine superintendent. Lived in the big house beyond yours, he did, and I did his chores. Well, so long as the whores minded their own business and kept out of sight, nobody minded them much. Fact is, some felt having that old whorehouse there kept the jacks from tearing up the whole town when they come out of the woods. But one afternoon, when their madam was away, three of the girls, all painted up like Injuns, had the nerve to walk all the way up the street giggling and carrying on fierce like, a-wiggling their butts at any man they passed. Couldn't much blame them, it being a nice spring day, but the people sure got plenty mad and they told Thompson something had to be done about it." The cowbell clanked again.

"There's another old bullhead swallered a hook for sure," he said. "Well, as I was a-saying, something had to be done so Henry Thompson, he strapped on his forty-five an' told me to come along down there with him about the time the St. Paul train was due. He just bust in the door and laid down the law. Told the madam and the whores he was putting them on the train for Green Bay. Right then. No stalling. Wouldn't let them say a word, come as they were. Leave everything. Henry, he give the madam a hard slap across the face when she tried to give hime some lip and we had no more trouble. Got 'em on the train and waited till it pulled out. That Henry Thompson, he were quite a man, yes sir. They used to call him King of Tioga..."

"But the haunts, Dick? What about the haunts?"

"Coming to that," replied the old man and he filled and lit an old corncob pipe, knowing he had us hooked good.

"Well, 'bout a month or so after that, Henry Thompson, he got some men and sent them down to board up the house tight so there'd be no more trouble. Nail down the windows too, he said, before you board them. Well, the men could nail down the windows downstairs from the outside but they had to go in to do them above. When they climbed the stairs they smelled a helluva rotten stink coming from a locked closet, and when they opened it, a dead women was there, all in a heap. I suppose the madam had locked her in to punish her. Maybe she was fixing to run away. I dunno. Anyway, she was left in that there closet and died there. They buried her out back of the house and nobody said nothing, knowing Thompson would get them if they did. You never hear that story boys? Well, it's true. I was one of them men and I know."

Dick poured another can of coffee before he went on. Well, her haunts been hangin' around the place since. I hear her ascreaming one night when I passed by and there's been others too as has heard her. Ask Old Pullapin. Damn near scared him out of his shoes. He said he saw lights in the house too, lights shining through the cracks in the boards but he'd been drinking so I dunno. I never seen no lights. No haunts, hey? You boys go down there some dark night and you'll find out. That old whore, she'll still be a screeching so loud you'll pee in yer pants."

As Mullu and I left, we could hear him muttering, "No haunts, hey? No haunts? They's lots of haunts every place."

The next afternoon Mullu came over to our house and made me a proposition. "Let's you and me go explore that old whorehouse tonight," he said. "You bring your dad's claw hammer and pry iron and I'll bring a candle and some matches. Nobody has to know. It'll be dark by eight o'clock and it shouldn't take long just to look it over. Maybe we'll see or hear that ghost."

I confess I didn't much like the sound of it but he shamed me into saying yes. So down the street we went and out along the slaughterhouse road till we came to the last building on the right. Sure dark by then and black as tar. I jumped four feet when the board Mullu was prying off the back door let go with a screech. Sure spooky. We had a hard time getting all those old boards off and the door opened but finally we got in. Couldn't see anything until Mullu lit the candle and that made it even spookier, it flickered so. The house smelled of mildew and camp damp. Rats or porcupines had sure messed it up something awful. I was all for getting out but no, Mullu said, we had to go upstairs and see that closet where the whore was locked.

He led the way up the creaking stairs. When I stepped on some loose plaster that had fallen off the stair well and it crunched, I jumped again. Then I heard something. "Mullu!" I whispered. "There's something down there below us. I just heard something moving. Listen!"

We listened hard, holding our breaths. "Aw, you're just imagining," Mullu said. I knew I wasn't. I'd really heard something rustling. Probably a rat but it sounded bigger. All my nerve endings were quivering.

"C'mon. Let's go, Cully." Mullu began to climb up the rest of the shaky stairs and I followed the candle he held before him.

There were several bedrooms up there, all interconnected by doors, and each had a cot and a chair, not much else. Some of the mattresses had fallen off and split open, or had been chewed open, for the wood shavings that filled them had spilled out of the openings and were all over the floors.

"Where's the closet?" Mullu whispered. We groped around trying to find it and finally did between the last two bedrooms. We had just stumbled over its fallen door and were trying to look inside when suddenly we heard a woman scream.

Geez! We were petrified, frozen in our tracks. I felt the hair on my scalp crawling. Then it screamed again, a woman in mortal agony. Mullu dropped the candle and it went out!

I still don't know how we managed to find our way down those ramshackle stairs in the blackness. Then, just as we were bursting out through the door, we heard a third scream - and a rifle shot so close it almost split our ears.

I don't know who ran faster, Mullu or me. All I know is that there were two exhausted kids panting on the platform of the depot trying to catch our breath before we started up the hill for home. Old Dick Duggan was right. There were haunts. And when I got home I went straight to bed with the covers over my head, trying to forget what had happened.

The next day we had to go to school. Mullu and I didn't look at each other. Sure was hard to concentrate, the memory of that woman screaming was so vivid. I found myself shuddering, just thinking about it.

It being the opening day of school, we didn't have to go in the afternoon so when Dad suggested I go with him as he made his calls, I was glad to accept even though it meant a lot of waiting in the buggy while he was in the houses. When he came out of the last one after a long, long time, Dad said, "Mrs. Laroux just told me that LaSeur shot a big Canadian lynx last night. Let's go over and see it. I've only had a glimpse of one in my whole life. They're getting scarce but I've heard them several times when I've been out hunting or fishing. They sound like a woman in childbirth who's having a rough time of it. A real screech. Once Jim Johnson and I were sleeping overnight up by the Hayshed Dam and had our baskets of trout hanging from some bushes by the fire when a lynx let out a howl and screech that sure jumped us out of our blankets. I suppose he was after the fish but you've never heard a scream like that, I'll bet."

When we got to LaSeur's cabin, Dad explained that he wanted me to see the lynx. LaSeur led us out to his barn. The animal looked like a gigantic grey and white cat with a big head and whiskers. In the middle of its brow, right between the eyes, was a bullet hole.

Dad grinned and so did LaSeur. "Yeah, Doc. I know what you're thinking. Yeah, I was headlighting for deer last night over by the slaughterhouse and I see green eyes, not yellow like deer, but I shoot and get this cat. A big one, eh Doc?" Dad agreed.

I told Mullu about it next day and he said maybe so, maybe what we'd heard was that lynx. But he also said later that he had gotten a bullhead from Dick Duggan and nailed it over the door of the haunted whorehouse when he went back there to get our claw hammer and pry bar.

AUNT LIZZIE: EVANGELIST

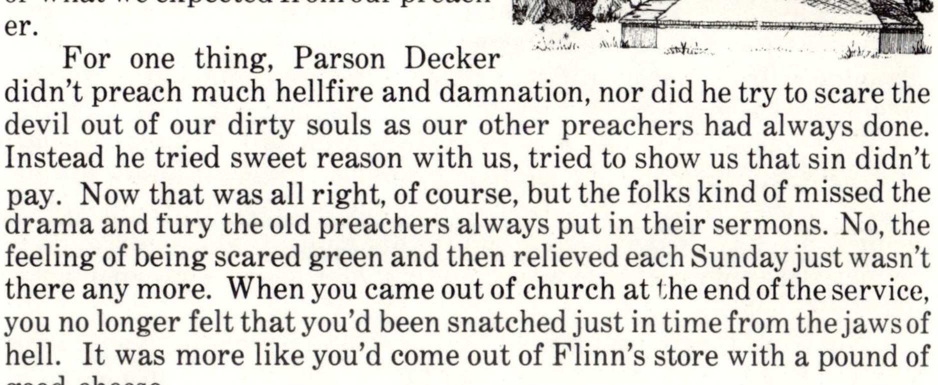

I think it was in the fall of year 1913 that we got William Decker, the new young preacher from down below. Before he'd run out his time with us they were calling him Decker the Wrecker. That wasn't really fair because he was a nice young fellow with plenty of good intentions and enthusiasm. The trouble was mainly that he didn't know us or how we lived or what we expected from our preacher.

For one thing, Parson Decker didn't preach much hellfire and damnation, nor did he try to scare the devil out of our dirty souls as our other preachers had always done. Instead he tried sweet reason with us, tried to show us that sin didn't pay. Now that was all right, of course, but the folks kind of missed the drama and fury the old preachers always put in their sermons. No, the feeling of being scared green and then relieved each Sunday just wasn't there any more. When you came out of church at the end of the service, you no longer felt that you'd been snatched just in time from the jaws of hell. It was more like you'd come out of Flinn's store with a pound of good cheese.

For another thing, Mr. Decker was too evangelical for most of our folks. Often he seemed to be more interested in saving other people's souls rather than our own. Our congregation felt that if they paid a preacher, he should take care of their souls exclusively, not start trying to persuade old Pete Halfshoes, our half-breed Indian, to quit drinking and come to church. They knew that if Pete did come, he'd bring his pet skunk, Mabel, with him and they'd both be snockered good.

Nor did his parishioners like it when Mr. Decker tried to raid the congregations of the other churches in town by getting their kids to come to his Sunday School so they could play baseball on our team Saturday afternoons. That wasn't right! Over the years our village had achieved a fairly stable truce between the Catholics, the Lutherans, the Methodists, and even the Holy Jumpers. A man's religion, if he had any, was his own business, and if he didn't have any religion at all, well, that was all right too. Live and let live!

When I got home one evening singing a new song we'd learned at Epworth League, even my father was a bit upset. "That man's going to make trouble in our community," he said to my mother. Mother hadn't heard me singing it so I sang it again. It had a good tune.

"Oh, the foxes they got holes in the ground,
And the birds got nests in the air,
And everything's got a resting place,
But a sinner ain't got no where.
Oh, there's great trials,
Grand tribulations.
There is great trials,
I'm bound to leave this land.
"Oh, Methodist, Methodist is my name,
Methodist 'till I die,
I'm going to join the Lutheran Church,
But I'll die on the Methodist side.
Oh, there's great trials,
Grand tribulations.
There is great trials,
I'm going to leave this land."

When some of the elders tried to calm Mr. Decker down on his proselitizing, they just made him more determined. So one Sunday, he announced from the pulpit that three Sundays from that date, they would have a very special service, an evangelical one. Every church member was to bring another person to church with him. Mr. Decker said he would prefer that we bring persons who had never gone to church in their lives or who had dropped out, but it would be all right to bring someone who belonged to some other church too. There would be stars in the crowns of those who brought two or more. You can imagine how that shook us up.

Not Aunt Lizzie, though. As a pillar of our church, she wanted that star and that crown. She'd bring her quota, she said. Mean, old gossip that she was, Aunt Lizzie had always been a consistent church goer. Never missed a Sunday. Some people said it was only so she could do her bloody screeching in the choir. Aunt Lizzie was awful on those high notes, clinging to them, flatting or sharping them, torturing the hell out of them till all of us shriveled in our seats. I don't know why they didn't kick her out of that choir, she made us suffer so, but probably they feared her nasty tongue. Lately, she'd been singing solos only once in a while and that was a mercy. At least she didn't spoil the grand old hymns, thanks to Annie, our organist, who drowned her out.

Aunt Lizzie did a lot of thinking before she settled on Eino Tuomi and Emil Olson as the two sinners she'd bring to church that evangelical Sunday of Sundays. Lord knows, they qualified! Those two old whiskey drinking reprobates had never been to church in their whole lives. Probably hadn't even been baptized either. Aunt Lizzie realized that it would take some real careful scheming to come to church with those two trophies.

The next morning when I brought her the weekly copy of *Grit*, Aunt Lizzie had notes for me to deliver to both old men. Since Emil couldn't read and I knew I'd have to read his note to him anyway, I unfolded it. "Dear Mr. Olsen," it said, "I have some work I need done. If you can help me on Wednesday and Friday mornings I will pay you. Sincerely, Mrs. Elizabeth Campton." Eino's note was the same but she'd asked him to come work for her on Tuesday and Thursday mornings. That puzzled me a bit as I walked down to their houses. Those two old buggers were almost like brothers. They were inseparable. Why, they even ate together although they lived in separate houses side by side at the bottom of the hill. They shared their garden, the milk from Eino's cow, and the eggs from Emil's hens. You never saw one of them without the other - even when they were out poaching deer.

Emil and Eino sure needed the work. Winter would soon be coming and the potato crop had been poor that year. They wouldn't have had any potatoes at all except that they'd gone up to the town hall and emptied all the spittoons to make bug juice. Oh, they had enough turnips but you can get sick of turnips day after day. Worst of all, neither of them had been able to store up any whiskey for the long winter. All they had between them was one bottle of red-eye and that was being saved for New Year's Eve if they didn't break down and drink it before. In other years, Emil and Eino had always counted on the money they got for sawing the wood for the Town Hall's stoves to buy their booze, but this year the damned Township Board had given the contract to Sam Ysitalo. The thought of a long winter without whiskey was unsettling.

Therefore, promptly at eight o'clock that next Tuesday morning, Eino was at Aunt Lizzie's house ready to do whatever she wanted done. She greeted him more warmly than he'd expected she would. "Thank you, Eino," she said. "I hoped you come help a poor widow lady. Come in and have a cup of coffee while I tell you your job this morning." She also gave him a big slice of homemade bread with wild strawberry jam on it to go with the coffee. Eino hadn't had anything taste so good for years.

"I've got a lot of work that takes a real man to do," she said, "but first, I'd like to have you saw up that long cord of maple wood in the back yard. Stove length and split and piled in the shed." When Eino suggested that maybe he'd better go get Emil to help with the sawing she vetoed it. “No, Eino,” she said. “Just you. You’re a big handsome man and can do it yourself. There’s a one man crosscut saw in the barn and you’ll find the axe there too.”

Eino shrugged. Didn’t make any sense. Two men could saw a lot more a lot faster than one man could. But what the hell! The job would just last longer and he’d make more raha, more whiskey money. Eino worked hard all morning and had the logs cut up by noon even though that saw sure needed filing. When he came to the house for his pay, Aunt Lizzie inspected the woodpile,praised him effusively, and again had him in for coffee and fresh doughnuts. “No matter what they say about Aunt Lizzie,” Eino thought, “she’s a damned good cook.” But a moment later, when she put only a fifty cent piece in his outstretched hand, he was shocked and disappointed. He looked at it with his mouth open.

“Not much pay for a full morning’s work,” he said. Hell, that wasn’t enough for more than a good snort or two.

Aunt Lizzie saw his unhappiness. “Yes, Eino. That’s not enough wages, I know. But I’m a poor widow lady, Eino, and that’s all I can afford.” Somehow she squeezed a tear out of one eye while watching him with the other. “You’re a good man, Eino. Help me if you can.” The old Finn put the fifty cent piece in his pocket and left.

When Emil found out how little Aunt Lizzie had paid his friend, he was outraged. “You too easy going, Eino,” he roared. “No man work all morning for fifty cents. Tomorrow I tell her one dollar or she can stick it. We never get whiskey money that way.”

And Emil did tell her, too, next morning. Told her one dollar or nothing doing. Aunt Lizzie surprisingly gave in right away. Even gave him an extra fifty cents for Eino. Moreover, she also had him in for coffee and doughnuts after he’d split the chunks Eino had sawed the day before.

Well, that’s the way it went for the three weeks before Evangelical Sunday. Aunt Lizzie got a lot of work done out of those two. They cut up another long cord of wood and stacked it; they took down her stovepipes, shook the soot out of them, and put chains up and down her chimney. Emil cleaned her chickencoop and put down fresh fall leaves for the hens to scratch in. Eino made a big stack of new cedar kindling.

But Aunt Lizzie was good to them. The two old men had never had such good eating. Why, sometimes Aunt Lizzie even had a big slab of apple or blueberry pie for them after work and she didn’t seem to mind interrupting to get them to talk about themselves and their past lives. Somehow she seemed to be able to weasel out of them stuff they’d never even told to each other.

Of course, Aunt Lizzie talked too - often about church and religion and such. She seemed surprised, almost shocked, when they told her no, they’d never been in a church. She said that was too bad, that everyone ought to go to church at least once, that they were sure missing something. Finally, toward the end of the third week, after she had fed Eino a batch of cinnamon rolls fresh from the oven, she suggested that maybe he and Emil might go to church that next Sunday. She was going to sing a solo, she said, and she'd really like to have her boys hear it. Aghast at the thought, but trying to be polite,Eino said that he couldn't go because he didn't have any church clothes. Aunt Lizzie didn't argue. She understood, she said. "Have another cinnamon roll, Eino."

The next day she also brought it up to Emil who said the same thing, having been forewarned. Then Aunt Lizzie invited both her boys to come to have supper with her Saturday night. She'd really appreciated their help and wanted to do something special for them. Pot roast and all the fixings, she said. They accepted.

Ah, that was a good meal! Eino and Emil hadn't had one like that in their whole lives. Not only pot roast with browned potatoes and mashed rutabagas, but a side dish of chicken salad too. And then a big hunk of delicious coconut pie. A feast!

But that wasn't all. Aunt Lizzie went to the back room after the meal was over and brought out two men's coats, two pair of pants, two neckties, and two pair of men's shoes. "These are for you, dear boys," she said. "They were my past husbands' and they've been in the closet for years now. I've noticed that both your mackinaws and pants are pretty thin and with winter coming, you ought to have better ones. Besides, you said you couldn't come to hear me sing in church because you had no church clothes. Well, now you have them, my dear boys. You be there to meet me at the church door tomorrow at 10:45 or I'll come get you." Boom! Just like that!

Emil and Eino had been able to stash away five bottles of whiskey by that time and they emptied one of them that night. Still a bit hung over next morning, they had a terrible time putting on the new clothes, especially those neckties around the collars of their old lumberjack shirts. They didn't even tackle the shoes. Splay footed from years of wearing clompers, they couldn't even get their toes in them. When Emil came over to Eino's house at ten-thirty, he found his friend all dressed up but sipping another hair of the dog. "I can't go, Emil," he said. "These damn store clothes driving me crazy."

But the two old men were at the church door at ten-forty-five, mainly because the thought of old Aunt Lizzie leading them up the hill was too horrible to consider. She was outside when they got there. Triumphant, she looked them over, straightened their ties, then led them in to shake hands with the young preacher. I was an usher that day but when I tried to lead them down in front, Emil said, "No, Cully. We sit in back!" And they did, in the last pew nearest the door, so I put Charley Olafson along the aisle in that pew to box them in. Emil and Eino really looked kind of nice in their new church clothes, but their eyes were sure scared. I couldn't help sneaking glances at them all through the service to see how they were doing.

Eino was slumped down, almost hiding, in his part of the pew but Emil was looking all around. When Annie Anderson started playing the organ, they both were so startled they jumped and Emil got to his feet to see better what she was doing. (He told me later that it was the first time he ever saw a woman walking while sitting down. He was referring to her pumping the foot bellows.) Then in walked our choir, three men and three women, and Aunt Lizzie. The two old men nudged each other but it wasn't time for the solo yet. Our choir's first number wasn't too bad. Billy Timmons, the bass, had a strong, low, vibrant voice and the tenor hit the high notes true enough. You couldn't say that for Aunt Lizzie but Annie managed to cover up those high screeches of hers pretty well.

Then came the Call to Worship and another hymn. That presented some problem. Emil and Eino had trouble knowing when to stand or sit, always doing both too late. Sort of out of sync. They watched the others pick up the hymn books and did so themselves but they didn't try to sing, of course. Emil couldn't read English, let alone music. Then after the preacher read a long passage from scripture about brotherhood, he said a long prayer about being each other's keepers and ended by blessing all the newcomers who were there that day. Emil and Eino hadn't been blessed before and they sort of liked it.

Next came the offering while the choir sang again. Emil looked startled when he saw the plates being passed around. "Hey, Eino! You got any raha?" he said in a loud whisper that made the people in front turn around slightly. Eino passed him that first fifty cent piece of Aunt Lizzie's to put in the plate and then didn't have anything else to put in, so he just pretended. A quick learner, Eino. Then came the Doxology with all the congregation saying it good and strong, another hymn, and finally the sermon.

Mr. Decker's text was something about bringing in the sheaves and he sure brought in too many of them. The sermon lasted a good half hour too long and before he was half through, Emil and Eino were wriggling around on those hard pews trying to get comfortable. Yes, and crossing and uncrossing their legs. They'd drunk too much whiskey the night before and had too much coffee before they got dressed. I could see them fighting for self control. It gets harder as you get older.

At last, at long last, when the preacher ended his sermon with another prayer, he announced that Mrs. Elizabeth Campton would render the solo entitled "Whispering Hope." She rendered it; she sure did. To the organist's surprise, Aunt Lizzie began in a key three notes too high. Annie did her best but she had a tough time trying both to transpose and to blot out with an organ blast those high notes of Aunt Lizzie's. It wasn't too bad on the first "whisper my dreams" but the second time around Annie just stopped playing altogether and Aunt Lizzie really butchered it good. Then, frowning, she stopped abruptly, waiting for the organ to catch up.

In that merciful moment of silence every person in the congregation heard Emil's hoarse whisper. "Excuze! Eino and me we got to go pee." Charlie Olafson moved his number fifteen shoes out of the way and out of the pew the two men shot, out of the church door, and around the back for relief.

But they didn't go to their houses right away. Instead, they went up to Aunt Lizzie's place, took off their ties and their coats, and after a moment's hesitation, the pants that had belonged to the husbands she had buried. Dumping everything on Aunt Lizzie's back steps, the two old buggers loped home down the long hill street. Fortunately, they'd got beyond the church when the people started coming out but I got a good look at them as they high-tailed it around the corner. Quite a sight they were in those lumberjack boots and long underwear!

When Emil and Eino got to their cabins they felt so virtuous they opened another bottle. That left three for the winter.

DR. SPRINGER

The crows are back! The crows are back!" The joyous shout echoed up and down our hill street. It had been a terrible winter, much worse than usual, with one great storm following another. Drifts piled upon drifts until some of our lower windows were half covered and our sidewalks were more tunnels than pathways. No January thaw had come our way that year, nor did February or March bring relief. LaTour, the oldest man in our village, said he'd never seen the likes of it in his lifetime.

But the crows had returned at last and there was joy in Tioga. "We've made it through the winter! We've made it through the winter!" That was what we said to ourselves over and over again, and what we said to everyone we met. Those unfortunates who have never experienced an Upper Peninsula winter cannot possibly understand the sense of triumph, rebirth and renewal that always was ours when spring finally came.

Day followed day with blue skies and warm sun. The drifts sagged; you could even see the tips of the picket fences piercing them. Saucers formed around the base of the maple trees; great loads of snow shuddered off the heavily laden firs. Although it still froze hard every night, rivulets and then torrents of water ran down our hill street. We kids made snow dams across it and were delighted when they broke and carried our stick boats away. All of us were wet to the bone until we went to bed but no one spanked us. It was spring, spring, spring, and everybody was smiling. The whole town of Tioga was full of laughter.

With the release came a great burst of energy. The men took down the storm windows and the storm sheds from in front of the doors. They cleaned out the barns and chicken coops. They tapped the maple trees. They trapped beaver and fished the open edges of Lake Tioga for trout or they dangled their lines from the railroad bridge over our river for the pike that were going up to spawn. They split summer wood. They greased their boots.

The women stopped counting the mason jars of venison and fruit in their cellars and went into a veritable orgy of housecleaning and baking. Mrs. Mattson was the first to hang out a line of clothes to flap colorfully in the soft breeze even though she had to wade in snow three feet deep to manage it. Other wives were soon doing it too.

Horses rolled in the barnyard with their feet kicking the spring air. Cows bellowed incessantly, and often played bull, mounting each other. Chickens began to lay again once they were freed to scratch in patches of brown grass outside their coops. Dogs roamed the yards in groups with lust in their souls. It was spring.

We kids were erupting volcanoes of energy too and our parents had to catch us to get us to sprout the rest of the potatoes and to haul them up from the cellar before it filled with melt water. We made snowmen and snow forts where we fought viciously with hard packed snowballs. We cleared out a space to play marbles. Out of shingles, we made boats with little paddlewheels powered by a rubber band and sailed them across the ever growing puddles. Why, we even enjoyed chopping big cakes of ice off the sidewalks with the splitting axe. Hard work, but each big chunk we could slide off the walk brought us closer to summer. School became almost unbearable. To be jailed inside when the birds were singing in the sun was torture. By the time the breakup was over, we had known more spankings for misbehavior than at any other time of the year. Who cared? Whoops! It was spring at last.

But there was one house in our village still filled with winter's gloom. In it lived Jacques and Marie Conteau, both in their late sixties. They were waiting to die. Not that there was anything really wrong with their health, my father said after a neighbor asked him to visit them, but they had no reason for living. The fall before, Jacques had sold his cow, and killed his chickens and two pigs because he was tired of tending them. "My strength, she is gone," he said. All Jacques had left was an old horse. He would have sold her too but no one wanted to feed it through the winter. Jacques had nothing to do nor any urge to do it.

Marie, throughout their forty years of married life, had often had spells of depression accompanied by mild and vague ailments that my father could not cure. Her husband, Jacques, like most French Canadians, had always been a gay spirit but it had been a long hard winter (tres dolouereux) and he too had been down in the dumps for a long, long time. The two of them rarely spoke to each other any more. After forty years, what was there to say? Silently, Marie prepared the meals, and silently they ate them without appetite or enjoyment. Jacques went to bed early and got up at dawn; Marie went to bed late and rose long after sun-up so they could escape each other. They slept on the edges of the bed as far apart as they could get.

Partly because the Conteau's house was the last one on the road to Mud Lake and the snowplow never went that far, Jacques and his wife had been pretty snowbound all winter. No one came to see them and Marie never left the house. Jacques did snowshoe into town once every two weeks for groceries or to get the mail but that was all. Usually they got a monthly check from their only child, a son who lived in California and hadn't been back for seven years, and this was what they lived on. Not that they ate much or needed much. The Conteaus didn't feel lonely; they just felt angry and depressed. Marie no longer braided her hair but wore it in a straggly bun and didn't care how she looked. She also sighed frequently and every time she did, it irritated her husband so much he thought of popping her one if she ever did it again. So he went out to the barn, fed and bedded the horse, and whittled fire sticks until he had enough for ten winters. The evenings were the longest and the worst. She read, or pretended to read, her Bible and he the Farmer's Almanac. Neither had smiled since the summer before.

Finally, about the middle of May, they had their first visitor. It was Francois Bourdon with whom Jacques had often fished and hunted. "The walleye are running, Jacques," he said. "Untu caught seven big ones last night off the railroad bridge. I got plenty of chub minnows. You come with me." But Jacques refused. He was not feeling well, he said. Francois was appalled to see how the two of them looked. Thin and sallow, with droopy mouths! The winter had been hard on them. They really looked sick so he came to our house and asked Dad to go see them.

When Dad returned he went down to see Father Hassel, the Catholic priest. "Father," Dad said, "what's the policy of your church about suicide?"

"It's a major sin, Doctor. Why do you ask?"

"Well," said my father, "two of your flock seem determined to commit it by slow attrition. The Conteaus. They're in bad shape, deeply depressed, not eating enough. Nothing really physically wrong with them but..."

"Come to think of it," interrupted the priest, "they haven't been to church or confession for over a year. I'll go to see them right away, of course, but what do you prescribe?"

"I deal with the body, Father," said Dad. "You deal with the soul. Their souls are sick, deathly sick. They'll never make it through the summer to say nothing of another winter. I've seen it happen. They've got to have some reason for living. They've got to have something to care for and love and they have nothing. I told them I'd send them some medicine and if you're going to see them soon, you might take this bottle with you. It's my own special concoction for a spring tonic. I call it the Elixir of the Root of the Royal Banyan Tree. Mostly alcohol, of course, and it tastes pretty good if I do say so, myself. You might try a nip of it yourself, my friend, if only to help you bear that ugly housekeeper of yours."

The priest grinned and accepted the large bottle. "I may just do that, Doctor." he said. "Or call upon you for another one for me."

As my father left, he said, "All foolishness aside, I'm really worried about the Conteaus. They've got to get some meaning and loving in their lives."

And so it came to pass that about a week later when Jacques went out to the barn to whittle some more fire sticks, he found in it a little springer spaniel puppy wiggling a tiny stub of a tail. Jacques rushed back to the house. "Marie, Marie!" he called. 'Come see! A little puppy is in the barn."

"A dog in the barn, a horse in the barn, you in the barn, so?" She didn't look up from her Bible and her voice was a listless monotone. It was the longest utterance he'd heard from her in months.

"I show you then." When Jacques picked up the little puppy to bring it into the kitchen, the dog licked his face and he noticed for the first time that there was a note with writing on it tucked under the collar.

"Marie, see what I find out there in the straw? You got glasses on. What this paper say? " He handed her the note. She read it twice before she answered.

"It say 'Dear Jacques and Marie: My name is Willie. I am six weeks old. I would like to live at your house. Also I am very hungry, please. A friend sent me to you.' "

"No," Marie said. "No! We will have no dog here. Put it outside or take back to barn. This no place for a dog. Or for you or for me. We too old and sick to have a young dog."

But Jacques put the puppy in her lap as he went to the cupboards. "We give Willie something to eat first," he said. "What you have for him. We got no milk, no meat, no bone. Two egg here. And bread. What we fix for Willie, Marie?" He noticed that she was holding the little dog in her arms as though it were a baby and that it was licking her thin hands.

"I fix something," she replied but when she gently put the puppy on the floor, it whined softly so she picked it up again and began stroking him. "Willie scared, I think," she added. "I hold him now some more. You make mash of egg and bread and canned milk and put in saucer." Willie began to climb up her body to lick her neck and as she brought the little dog down to cradle and cuddle him in her arms, Jacques noticed that she was smiling. He hadn't seen that smile for years. Old as she was, Marie was almost pretty when she smiled that way.

Willie was hungry and lapped up every bit of the food in the saucer. Then he went over to Marie's feet and promptly went sound asleep. The Conteaus looked at each other.

"What you think, Marie? Who bring the dog?"

"I don't know. Maybe Francois, eh? Or the Dumonts, may be so?" The puppy stirred and she stroked its back. Willie sighed and went back to sleep. "What we going to do? We don't want dog here. How we take care when we sick?"

Jacques thought for a long time and tried to keep from looking at the pup. "Yes," he said finally. "We go to town this afternoon and find out where he come from and give him back. You come too, Marie, to hold dog in the buggy. And put on that pretty pink dress and blue jacket so you look nice. I going to shave even."

Jacques spent most of the morning cleaning up and curry combing the old horse who was well caked with manure from the long winter. Marie washed and braided her hair. As they drove down the road to town in the warm spring sun, they both felt better than they had for a long time.

Francois wasn't home but his wife, Elsie, made them welcome. Of course, they had to have coffee and cinnamon rolls. The conversation was gay but no, Elsie was sure that Francois hadn't brought Willie. She made much of the puppy too and Willie loved the attention. Then the three of them went to the Dumonts and had to have coffee and cake again. No, no one in town had springer spaniels they were told. Lots of hounds but there wasn't a dog in town that looked like Willie. They visited several other old acquaintances and got the same story. At the last house, old Dewarre offered to take the puppy. "That's a fine dog," he said. "The best there is for partridge. I give you five dollars for him."

Jacques looked at his wife. "No," she said, "we'll find who give Willie to us or we keep him ourselves." The little puppy wiggled his tail and nuzzled her arms. Both of them hid their relief as they got in the buggy to go home. Neither said anything but it was decided. Wilie was their own.

They stopped at Flinn's store and cashed one of their son's checks to buy a big pot roast with a marrow bone in it, some milk, eggs and butter and a big bag of flour. As Marie gathered up the supplies, Jacques wandered around the store. "Marie, you come here. I buy you new hat so you look pretty, yes?" He held Willie while she tried them on. When they left the store, she was radiant and both of them were almost happy. As they clopped, clopped along the road home, Jacques found himself humming the old song: "Oh, zee wind she blow from zee north/and the wind zee blow some more/but you won't get drown in Lac Champlain/so long as you stay on zee shore."

That night Jacques suddenly awoke to find that Marie was not in his bed. Nor was she downstairs. He found her in the barn sitting on a bale of hay rocking Willie. "I hear him crying," she said. "He scared and much alone so I come. Look, he sleep now." Jacques went back to bed but it was a long time before Marie did too.

Thanks to Willie, the summer was a delight to both of them. He changed their lives completely. For one thing, there was always something to talk about. Willie had chased a bee and got stung. That was why he'd come ki-yiing back to the house. He also got burrs in his ears that only Marie could remove as she bathed him in sweet talk. Willie had brought back a stick Jacques had thrown into a puddle. Should she, Marie, give Willie a bath? He was scratching a lot. She was concerned. Willie had got so far down in a fox hole only his tail was showing and Jacques had found it hard to get him back out. That sort of talk. There was always something to say to each other.

Now that they were going to church and confession again, they hated to lock Willie in the barn when they were gone. Jacques just had to build a fence, Marie said. And a doghouse too where she could put the sleeping pad she'd made from an old quilt. It was good to hear the sewing machine going again, Jacques thought, and to have his socks mended and buttons sewed on but he sort of hated to fence Willie in. Such a gay spirit in that dog. And how affectionate he was, always ready to run in joyous circles when it looked as though Jacques was going to take him for a long walk. Always ready to jump into Marie's lap if she sat on the back steps or on the cellar door. Willie was getting bigger now. Big feet and long legs. Soon he'd overlap that lap of hers.

When the Conteaus had to have a fence or stay home all the time, Jacques repaired the woven wire surrounding the old pig yard and pig house. Marie didn't approve even though a heavy crop of grass and weeds had come up in it. "Willie too nice a dog for pigpen," she said. She didn't give in until Jacques had cut the weeds and grass with his scythe and put a new floor in the pig house. But Willie didn't like it either. He didn't like it at all! He ran around the enclosure and howled so long Marie had to go inside the fence to comfort him. And then he howled some more when she left. "He get used to it," said Jacques.

Marie was delighted when the howling suddenly stopped and discovered a very proud but dirty Willie on the back steps wagging his tail. He had dug a hole under the gate so Jacques buried a length of fencing and put Willie back. How the dirt flew between the mournful howls, but finally the puppy lay down in the sun and slept. A half hour later, however, he was back on the steps again. No, Willie hadn't dug his way out but the gate was open. Jacques put him back again and peeked around the corner of the barn. The dog was pushing up hard with his nose against the bent wire latch and soon had dislodged it from its staple. "He's smart dog," Jacques told his wife, "But I'm smarter." He installed a throw-bolt on the gate. "Now, let's see you get out!" he said as he went back to the house. Oh, the wailing! But ten minutes later, there was Willie on the steps again even though the gate was still locked. Impossible! Jacques put him back and watched again, this time to see Willie climb that five foot fence and flop over its top. That was the end of his being fenced in. Thereafter when the Conteaus left the house, Willie was first shut up in the barn, then later, in the summer kitchen.

Feeding was no problem. Willie ate what they did except for fresh peas which he picked out of the dish and dropped on the floor. An egg beaten up with milk and bread was his favorite so Jacques bought a cow and then chickens. A lot more work, but somehow it seemed enjoyable. Willie went along when Jacques drove the Jersey to the pasture and again when he went after her. At milking time the dog sat beside Marie, waiting for his saucer of warm milk. Both Jacques and Marie talked constantly to the dog, Willie cocking his ears and listening intently. He even understood French Canadian and would come immediately when Jacques whistled with forefingers between his teeth and yelled "Venez, Willie, Venez!"

As his second teeth began to come in, the dog chewed anything it could find. Chunks of wood, a tin can, anything. A new soup bone was soon whittled down to a scrap. Marie rubbed his red gums with a forefinger. Willie didn't bite. In August month Jacques went hunting again and shot an illegal deer so Willie could have plenty of bones and meat and Marie canned the venison for the winter. When Francois brought them a fine mess of trout, they discovered that Willie couldn't get enough of the pink meat so Jacques began to fish again, too. The dog wasn't much good when Jacques had to wade the stream for it loved the water and would spoil the holes with its splashing so Jacques borrowed Francois' boat and trolled for pike in Lake Tioga. Willie would sit on the back seat, stiff and erect, as Jacques rowed. "Mon Capitain!" Jacques called him. When a pike was thrashing in the bottom of the boat, the hills around the lake echoed with Willie's barking.

Willie also put on a frenzy of barking when Jacques cut down a tree for the winter's wood. As it fell, the dog would run around it in circles, then climb up on the fallen trunk and bay almost like a hound. "That dog, he think he chop it down himself," Jacques told Marie. And on the way home from the woods, Willie would sit on the wagon seat close beside the man, occasionally licking his face. Good company, that dog.

The spaniel was very affectionate. Willie loved everybody who came to the house and the Conteaus had a hard time for a while trying to stop him from getting in their laps too. They were having a lot of visitors once again by this time, not only the older people who stopped in for coffee and a chat, but a lot of kids too. Willie loved children of all sizes, especially when they'd throw a stick or chase him around the yard. "He's no watchdog, Marie!" said Jacques, but then of course, none of us needed a watchdog. No one in town ever locked their doors.

Soon it was fall and the pink fireweed and yellow goldenrod were in bloom everywhere. A few maple trees were gowned in scarlet. Jacques then took Willie hunting partridge, wandering the edges of hills and swamps where the yellow poplars grew. The dog roamed back and forth before him and when it spotted a grouse, it first froze and that stub of a tail vibrated swiftly. Then Willie began to jump stiff legged until the big bird flew up in a flurry of noisy wingbeating. Unlike most springers, however, Willie barked. Jacques was delighted.

You need a barking dog because if you have one, a partridge will fly up into a nearby tree and sit there looking at the dog and become an easy shot. Ah, that Willlie was a treasure.

By October, when the nights became cold, Willie was living and sleeping in the summer kitchen. There had been no problem with housebreaking either. Both Jacques and Marie just made sure that one of them always took him outside first thing in the morning and last thing at night, and always a half hour after he'd been fed. Only once had Willie had an accident and then he was so ashamed over the lapse that neither Jacques or Marie had the heart to punish him. Not that they ever had, for that matter. He was a good dog, Willie was. He never tried to enter the kitchen even when the door was open. He'd come to the threshold and look at them with his sad brown eyes but he wouldn't come a bit further. Indeed, when the weather got really cold, the Conteaus had a hard time convincing Willie that it was all right to go to his bed quilt under the kitchen table next to the big kitchen range. Somehow he seemed to know that it was a real privilege and was careful not to abuse it. Willie never begged for food at the table and when they snapped their fingers he always went right to his bed and lay there. Un bon chien!

One of the things that Willie had never mastered was climbing steps, even those that led up to the back stoop. If Marie was sitting there, he'd leap them to nuzzle her and beg to be scratched, but he wouldn't climb. Since the Conteaus rarely used the living room off the kitchen, Willie never entered it. Nor did he ever attempt to climb the steps in the open stairwell that led from it to the bedroom loft under the roof where they slept.

That was why, one very cold midnight in November,that Jacques was so surprised when he found Willie nudging him over from the edge of the bed towards its middle. Full of sleep, Jacques threw the upper blanket over the dog and found himself next to the warmth of Marie's body. For the first time in many years, he took her in his arms. They lived happy ever after.

SPITTING

When I was a boy in the old U.P., spitting was an art, a science, and a necessity. It was a necessity because almost all of our men chewed tobacco or took snuff and you don't swallow the juice of either or you'll turn green. Most of them also smoked but not on the job . Filling and tamping and lighting a pipe wasted too much time. "Taking a five," our phrase for a short rest, was not particularly approved of by most straw bosses. A man was supposed to work hard and to keep at it until quitting time.

So our miners always carried a plug of chewing tobacco in their hip pockets, biting off a chunk now and then throughout their hard day to keep the chew going. So did our lumberjacks, although most of them preferred loose tobacco, mainly Peerless, that they bought by the pailfull. It made a bigger and better cud, they claimed, one that could last half a morning of sawing pine. The snow around every stump was speckled with brown from their saliva. Those who worked on the railroad were about equally divided between chewing plug and loose tobacco.

But even some of the professional people were known to chew tobacco or indulge in snuff. My father, the doctor , said he started in medical school to counteract the stink of formaldehyde that came from the cadavers he had to dissect. Our school superintendent used snuff and so did one of the itinerant preachers who held services in the Methodist Episcopal Church. What I'm trying to say, I guess, is that spitting wasn't considered particularly vulgar back then. If you chewed tobacco, you had to spit. It was as simple as that, and as necessary.

Of course, there were limitations. You weren't supposed to spit on the floor. Every public building had signs in gold letters: "No Spitting On The Floor By Order Of The Board of Health." And, unless you couldn't wait another instant, you didn't spit in the presence of lady school teachers or such. Also, you didn't spit on another man's shoes unless you wanted to fight him. I can't say we were always discreet about our spitting, but there were rules of sort, and we followed them.

When the brown juice got to flowing strong and the men were inside a building, they looked for the nearest spittoon. Our word for spittoon was "gabboon" and I don't know why. They were everywhere except in church. Every house had one. Some were brown colored steel with an originally white mouth but the best were made of brass. Cleaned and polished, you can't find a prettier sight than a big brass gabboon gleaming on a sunny floor. Some families even used them occasionally as flower pots. But the best thing about brass spittoons as compared to the steel ones was that they rang when you hit them fair and square. Not a big noise, but it was a clang just the same. You didn't hear it if you hit the outside of the gabboon - only when you pinged the top around the hole. That was always the target.

Usually it was only the men that chewed tobacco and needed the gabboons. Some of the old Finn women did smoke their corncob pipes of Peerless as they rocked beside the warm kitchen range and a few of them also chewed Copenhagen snoos, as snuff was called. I used to like to visit the Haitemas to see old lady Haitema daintily spit in her special blue coffee cup. (All the others were white!) There'd be a big bulge behind her lower lip as she nursed her snuff, and then, when it was time, the old gal would pick up the blue cup from the floor beside her, hold it up before her mouth at arms length with little finger delicately extended, and let go. Never missed once.

All of us boys, of course, had to imitate our elders, first by chewing the fluffy white flowers of Indian tobacco, and then later the real stuff. It was a rite of passage to manhood. A lot of us, including me, tried as hard as we could but never managed to make the grade. I could handle Indian tobacco, but every time I tried snuff or cut plug, I wiped out. Awful tasting stuff and, no matter how fast I kept spitting, the taste lingered for hours in my mouth even if I chewed rhubarb afterwards. In my desperate experimentation, I twice swallowed some of the juice and almost lost my insides. Although I've been smoking a pipe now for sixty-five years - a dirty, filthy habit that I love - I never did acquire the ultimate merit badge of adulthood.

I said earlier that spitting, in addition to being a necessity, was an art and a science in the old U.P. Yes, we admired a really good spitter. The distance champion in our area was a big Swede who lived over by Half-Way named Sven Anderson. His record was thirteen feet and eleven inches - achieved on a windless winter day. The best any other man managed was a mere eleven feet which was plenty good. Sven had a mouth big enough to hold a cud as large as a baseball and he also had good teeth. You've got to have good front teeth as well as a strong tongue to spit well.

However, a lot of our men didn't have good teeth because they'd cracked too many hazelnuts in their youth and because there was no dentist nearer than Marquette. Filling a cavity was unknown and if you got a bad toothache, you either put some cotton soaked with oil of cloves on it, or you endured it, or you had someone pull it with a pair of pliers. No anesthetic! I vividly remember my father putting his forceps in my mouth and yelling, "Cully, hold onto that porch pillar tight and stop yelling!"

Anyway, many of our men didn't have the dental equipment to be a real spitting champion. Henry Nyman, though, was a fair to middling spitter and he hadn't had a tooth in his head for years. His gooms (gums) had so hardened that he didn't need teeth. I myself once saw him bite off a chunk of a black rye hardtack and chew it down without even wetting it. Some people claimed that one time Henry got in a fight and bit off the fellow's ear with those gooms. So I don't know if teeth really had anything to do with being a good spitter. Maybe it was just an art, handed down from father to son.

But it was also a science of sorts, especially when you tried for accuracy instead of distance. You had to calculate the right quantity and thickness of the juice in your mouth, how much air pressure to store up, and how suddenly to let it go. It wasn't just the velocity or the trajectory either. Often you had to figure in the windage.

The most accurate spitter we had in our forest village, but only at a distance of four feet, was Eric Niemi, who lived in a shack by Mud Lake. He's the one who never cleaned his trout. Just squeezed them till they squeaked and put them in the pan. Anyway, old Eric sure was accurate in his spitting. We kids liked to go down to his shack in the summer just to watch him nail flies to the panes of his one window with a good squirt of tobacco juice. Didn't have much of a view out of that window anyway because it looked over a swamp.

Because of the skill involved, all of us boys did a lot of spitting and we had to practice religiously to be good at it. We'd get a board with a knothole, draw a line on the ground to stand on, and try to spit through the hole without spattering the board, or we'd get a can to serve as a gabboon. For some reason, Mullu was usually more accurate than most of us and that was surprising because he spit a curve. He couldn't help it, he said, but he sure could hit the hole or the can most of the time. Most of us spit straight for the target but I found I could do best by lobbing it.

We also played a spitting game called Spimoryette. If a naive or newcomer boy came to play with us, we initiated him. "It's an old French Canadian game," we'd tell the poor devil. "Put your cap on the ground, turn around and cover your eyes and holler "Spimoreyette" seven times, and then we'll hide and you have to find us. Anyone you catch will be IT next time around." So the poor gullible kid would put down his cap and as he said "Spimoryette" (spit more yet) we'd follow his orders. We also had a game called "Peemoryette", but I won't describe that!

And, of course, in school we had spit balls. We usually didn't spit them though. We either used a blowgun made of a hollow elderberry stalk or a little gun of the same material with a spring made of a corset stay. You sure could make another kid yelp when he got hit in the neck by a spit ball from either of these. We also used to make a juicy spitball and plaster it onto the ceiling over the teacher's desk and watch with innocent anticipation until it dried and fell down on her head.

We even had a song about spitting. It went like this:

Oh, I'm a jolly consumptive,
Hawk, hawk, ptuie!
I do not work; I do not play.
All I do is spit all day,
Hawk, hawk, ptuie!"

But I've got to tell you about Maggie O'Conner, the cleaning lady at our railroad depot. All of us in Tioga were proud of that depot because it was a good sized one, being at the junction of the north-south and east-west railroads. There were four rooms in it. The western room was the place where all the American Express or Wells Fargo packages were stored as they came in. The next room was where the station master reigned and the telegraph operator worked and listened to the constant clattering of his keys. Then came the passenger waiting room with seats, the ticket window, and the board that told which trains were due and when. Finally, at the eastern end, was the baggage room. Only the two middle rooms were heated by potbellied coal stoves.

Maggie's job was to keep all of these rooms reasonably clean. The express and baggage rooms weren't too bad for Maggie but the middle two rooms were, especially the waiting room. Plenty of snow and dirt was always being tracked in there but the worst part of her cleaning job was due to the regular evening spitting competition to see who could hit the gabboon.

You see, there wasn't much to do in the evenings in our town. No TV or radio and few newspapers or reading material. Our men, if they had biting money, nursed a long beer at Higley's Saloon, but if they had none, Callahan's Store or the depot were about the only places they could go.

Somehow the men who regularly hung out at the depot in the evening started a spitting contest to see who could hit the top of the brass spittoon and make it ring. Every night there would be four or five of them, each of whom would put a penny in a can for the privilege of making a try for it. Whoever made the spittoon ping got the pot. At first they started from a chalked line about five feet away from the gabboon and then each night thereafter the distance was lengthened a foot. As you can imagine, there were more misses than hits and Maggie got sick of having to clean up the mess when the doors were locked at 9:30 after the last passenger train had left. She usually cleaned and mopped the floors of the express and baggage rooms first, then the station master's room and last of all the waiting room where the contest was held. When Maggie gave the spitters a piece of her mind for spitting all over the floor, the men said, "Aw, shut up, Maggie. That's yer job!" And when she appealed to the station master, he said the same thing. It was not a woman's world down there in the depot.

Finally, one night there was a lot of misses. In fact, because none of the men were able to hit the gabboon from seven feet, there were thirty-five pennies in the can. Maggie, who had been watching them, waiting with her mop, suddenly said, "Let an Irish woman try it!" and on the first attempt she let fly and pinged the gabboon right plumb on its top. As the men's mouths hung open, she picked up the spittoon and the can with the money, and left in triumph.

As you can imagine, the news of her feat spread throughout the village. For once, a woman had showed up the men in their most macho sport, and that without even having any tobacco juice to spit. "How did you do it Maggie?" one of her friends said. "Ah, it was easy," she replied. "I practiced a bit after closing time before I scrubbed the place and last night when I won the pot, they never knew I spit a raisin!"

That was the end of the evening spitting contests in the Tioga depot.

CALLAHAN'S STORE

(Parental Guidance Requested)

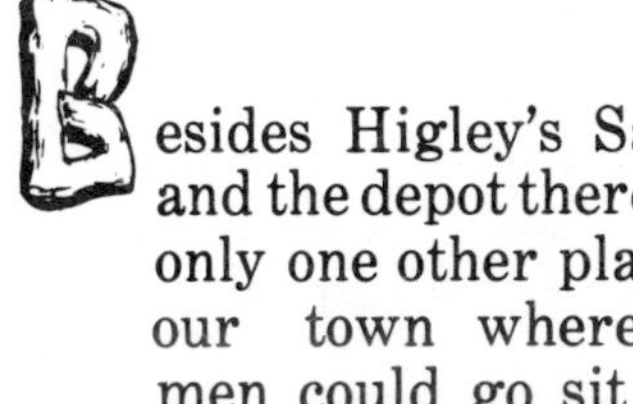esides Higley's Saloon and the depot there was only one other place in our town where our men could go sit on a winter's evening. That was Callahan's store which kept open until nine or ten at night, the store where the Last Man Under the Table poker club used to meet before they held that wake with drunken Dinny in the coffin. It was always warm there by the big pot bellied stove and usually four or five men could be found around it, sitting on boxes or cracker barrels, passing the time till Mike Callahan kicked them out and closed up for the night. Some wild stories were sure told around that stove.

There was the one about how in the old days the lumberjacks used to try to leave their mark on the low ceiling of the bunkhouse by jumping and kicking it with their sharp caulked (corked, they called it) boots. It took a good man to do it and many tried and failed. But there was one jack named Long Legs Poulet who gave a great leap, turned a somersault in the air, and planted both boots up in the pine boards so deep that they left him up there for three days to cure.

"Yah," someone said, "They was real he men in them old days. Had to be. A rough life that, logging the big pine and hauling them back over them hills. Why, there was one hill over beyond Hell's Canyon so steep they had to run a big rope over the top and hitch three span of oxen to pull the teams over the top." "Yeah," said one of the listeners, "I heerd of that hill. My pappy called it the five fart hill, because it took that many from his horse to get his buckboard over it."

"Speaking of farts," another man said. "Ever hear about how old man Mullen married him a young wife, 'cause he wanted a kid so bad. And he tried and she tried but nothing happened for a long time. And then she began to swell up good and the old man was sure proud and happy. Sure was nervous though when her time came due. Old man Mullen, he was a pacing up and down front of the bedroom door until Dr. Gage finally comes out. 'What 'tis it, Doc? Boy or a girl, Doc?' The Doc he give it to him straight, he did. 'Mr. Mullen,' he said, 'you sir, are the father of a ten pound fart!' "

"Yeah," said another man. "Doc Gage tells it to you straight. No beating around the bush or using ten pound words. Like the time the young preacher come to him with gonorrhea and tells him he caught it in an outhouse. 'Young man,' Doc sez, 'That's no place for intercourse!' "

"Speaking of preachers or priests," the first man said, I once got a young priest to save his soul, I did. I was coming up on the train from Milwaukee. Been visiting my daughter down there. Well, any old how, this young priest, still wet behind the ears, he gets on at Green Bay and sits down besides me. So I sez, 'Howdy, Mister. Nice day' just to be sociable like. But he wasn't having any of it. Didn't even nod. Just set there reading his Bible or something. Didn't say a damned word and kept way over on the end of the seat. I seen though that when any gal or woman walks up the aisle he looked 'em up and down and all over. Well, when we come to Iron Mountain, and he gets ready to get off, he turns to me and sez 'I fear I have not been a very good companion, sir, I am a man of the cloth and must do my devotions.'

"I give him a terrible glare, rose up from my seat and sez, 'Mebbe it's just as well, young man. For you see, *I AM THE DEVIL!'* Gadamighty, you should have seen the squirt gallop down the aisle a-crossing himself. Why, he was still doing it out on the platform when the train pulled out. Done a good deed, that day, I did!"

Of course, there always was a Paul Bunyan story or two. Like the one about how when Paul Bunyan had to take a crap, he always wiped his tail with thirteen porcupine. Damned near cleaned them out of the country in blackberry time. Once Paul could only find twelve so he sits down in the middle of Lake Tioga to clean himself and the water in the river runs upstream and spilled over the divide of land into Lake Superior. Damned poor trout fishing for three years.

The room was cooling off and one of the men began to put a big chunk of coal in the stove. "Hey, you!" hollered Mike Callahan. "Don't put that coal on. It's nigh closing time. If you're cold, go home!"

The man put the chunk back in the scuttle. "Jeez, for stingy!" he exclaimed. "Bad as that McGregor feller from Scotland who used to live in Republic. Stingiest man ever hit the bush, he was. They say that when his wife was in labor he got an old Finn midwife instead of the Doc. And when the baby starts coming, the Finn woman hollers at him, 'Turn up the lamp. I can't see!' So he did and the baby was born. Then McGregor turned down the wick again. 'Wait a minute, Mister,' she yells at him. 'Here comes another!' And out comes its twin, so he begins to turn down the lamp. 'Hold it!' she sez. 'Mebbe there's another!' 'Like hell,' says McGregor. He blew out the lamp and lit a candle. 'Damn light seems to attract them!' "

It was time to go home.

FLY TIME

Paradise had its snake and the U.P., that lovely land, has its insects: mosquitoes, black flies, gnats, deer flies, fish flies, horse flies and no-see-um-big-feelums. Often it didn't seem quite fair to have made it through a terrible winter only to have to endure fly time, that elastic period from the middle of May to the middle of July. Fortunately, there usually were a short few weeks after the break-up when we could roam the woods and streams unbedeviled by the flying hordes that would beset us later.

A good time that! Though little patches of snow still remained on the north sides of our granite hills and in the cedar swamps, the skies were bright blue and you could feel the warmth of the sun on your back as you knelt to smell the arbutus. We always knelt, perhaps as an unconscious posture of thankful prayer, but mainly to make sure that the arbutus we picked was truly fragrant. The pink kind was usually best but the white occasionally was most fragrant of all and there was always some arbutus that had no scent whatever. So we knelt and buried our winter faces in spring and brought home great bunches to give to our mothers or to sell to the passengers at the railroad depot.

Depending upon the season, this grateful period lasted only two or three weeks. Then, after a few warmer days, came the black flies, hordes of them, to swarm over our necks and faces, to climb up under our sleeves or pants, and sit there chewing away until, heavy with our blood, they dropped off to let others take their places. In a good year, according to Slimber, he'd counted one million to the acre in the open and more in the swamp.

Not only did black flies leave a bloody crust along your hairline, they also found their way into your nostrils, ears and the corners of your eyes. And your mouth, too. There were times when we inhaled through clenched teeth to prevent their entry when clouds of them surrounded our heads. Old Eric Lampi, who had a homestead on Mud Lake, almost went crazy when some black flies got inside his ear canal and fluttered there until my father squirted some peroxide into it and drowned them.

Couldn't really blame those black flies for getting in his ears. There was nowhere else to bite. Eric had hair down to his eyebrows and a heavy beard over the rest of his face. Actually, he looked like a very dirty teddy-bear. The flies probably tried his nose and hands first but these had a lot of yearly layers of dirt so hardened that nothing could penetrate the armour. Eric didn't believe in saunas or washing. "Water's for kalla (fish)," he said.

Those that got up your nose couldn't be wiped out; you had to blow them. My Dad was good at it. He'd take his nose between thumb and forefinger and with a mighty snort, would fling the contents to the ground. No handkerchief! Dad didn't use handkerchiefs except when there was company around. He always said that a rich man put in his pocket what a poor man threw away.

When the black flies were really thick, you also had to be careful when you took a leak out in the woods. The best way was to unbutton your pants and poke your pecker just a little way out through the slit and keep fanning the air with your other hand. Must have been tough on the women.

Since black flies, unlike mosquitoes, gave no warning and would be sitting and chawing on your neck before you knew it, most of us who wandered the woods developed a curious stroking gesture to clean them off our hides. You wiped your forehead, then the back of your neck and ears on one side with one hand, then did the same on the other side and you'd do it about once every minute. Got to be almost habitual after a time. They said that Jacques Poulin got so he was still doing it when snowshoeing.

Most of us wore a couple of large bandannas when we were trout fishing even though it was considered a sissy sort of thing to do. Sometimes we'd hide them in our pockets until nobody was around and then we'd put on one bandanna so it hung down from our hats in the back and on both sides, with one corner coming out in front till it hit our noses. Since it wiggled when we walked, that also discouraged any stray mosquito from settling too. The other bandanna we wound around our neck up to the chin. That gear really did seem to help but we always took it off when we got back to town. Like our parents, we kids in the U.P. were expected to be tough.

The gnats and no-see-ums came next. Gnats never really bothered us too much because they didn't bite. They swarmed all over us, of course, and got in our eyes and ears and we often inhaled them, but they were more of a nuisance than a real problem. Moreover, they didn't appear until after the sun got warm and they always went away at sundown.

No-see-ums were a different breed, however. So tiny they were almost invisible, they could bite like a chigger. Wiping them off didn't work; you had to scrape them. Even the bushiest beard didn't help for they worked their way through the underbrush and dug into the skin beneath. Fortunately, they too left at dusk, leaving their stings behind them to pester us for hours afterwards. Their surname of "big-feel-um" was sure deserved. Both gnats and no-see-ums bothered us worst when we were sweating and during the middle of the day. The only way we found to cope with the critters was to smear white zinc oxide over any exposed area and that made us look like Zombies. Most of us just endured them as the price we had to pay for being outdoors.

Mosquitoes came next, but I shall postpone telling about them until later. Some of our worst flies were deer flies. Looking like innocent house flies, except that they were gray, they didn't just drill us; they took out chunks of flesh. As we walked the trails up the Tioga River, they'd buzz around our heads in circles, and if you were quick enough you could catch them in the palm of your hand if you held your arm above your head. My brother Joe could catch them every time but they always seemed to light on the back of my hand rather than the front. Deer flies are at their worst in July and prefer hot, sunny days to do their deviltment. They seemed to inject an anesthetic so that you never felt their biting until after they've taken out a hunk of flesh and flown up onto a tree limb to digest it. No, deer flies don't hurt when they're biting, but they sure do afterwards. Deer and dogs as well as humans suffer a lot. The deer cope by splashing around at the edge of a lake and the dogs just rub their ears and nuzzles with their forepaws, moaning softly. No fly dope seems to deter deer flies.

In July, the fish flies arrived and they pestered us all summer long. They look just like ordinary house flies and perhaps they are but they bite like hell when you're in a boat or cleaning fish on shore. We usually carried fly swatters along when bass fishing because fish flies aren't hard to swat.

When I was a boy in the U.P. there were always a lot of horses and cows and therefore also a lot of horse flies. They could gouge out a real hole in your skin before you knew it. Almost an inch long and glossy black, it's impossible to swat them. In the old days, farmers or anyone else who owned horses covered their backs with a fringed leather netting that flopped around and dislodged them when the horses shook themselves. You can tell horse flies by their sound too. They have a booming buzz as well as a vicious bite.

But it's the mosquitoes for which the U.P. is most famed. These are not the namby pamby dwarfs that inhabit Lower Michigan or Wisconsin. Our mosquitoes are a different breed! They possess a hybrid vigor acquired over many generations of having to pierce the tough hides of tough people. They're a lot bigger too and we take a sort of perverse pride in them. To survive the bites of thousands of these supermosquitoes annually is to breed real character.

Unlike the sneaky black flies and deer flies, mosquitoes sound a warning before they attack. They are flying rattle snakes. At dusk by a lake or swamp you'll hear them howling like coyotes for blood, creating a universal tone that a musician friend of mine identified as C-sharp, but in a cabin at night a single mosquito as it zooms around your bed will vary its pitch. When the tone gets lower and louder, it means that the bugger's located its target and is ready to come in for a landing and to start drilling. It's almost impossible to swat or shoot them on the wing for they zag when you expect them to zig. You've got to wait there in the darkness with your skin quivering with tension until the skeeter finally lights and then you wait some more until it's too loggy to dodge when you slap at it hard. One mosquito in a bedroom is a lot but there will always be another one once you've thought you've got them all and have finally closed your eyes to sleep.

One of the first commandments every U.P. child learns at its mother's knee is not to scratch a mosquito bite no matter how much it itches. Scratching only makes the itch worse and often results in a swelling that can become infected. As boys we used to have competitions to see who could stand a drilling mosquito the longest. We'd bare an arm and then when one lit, we'd start counting. I remember one big black devil that drilled for a count of eighty-three and turned pink from my blood before it staggered away. Often, when we'd swatted a mosquito, you'd find a little patch of blood in your hand. We liked that; it was revenge! No wonder the people of the U.P. have *sisu*, that Finn word for being able to endure anything.

Oddly enough, mosquito dope was not taboo, although most of our men never used it. The basic standby was oil of citronella, a thin yellow liquid that you smeared on your ears, face, neck and wrists. My father used to buy it by the gallon and dispense it in four ounce bottles. We rarely put it on our foreheads because any sweat might run down to our eyes and the citronella in it would set them afire. Dad also had a big bottle of oil of pennyroyal for those who preferred that in their home-made concoctions. The worst fly dope was that used by LaTour, the oldest man in our village. He brewed up the worst smelling stuff of all, consisting of hot tar soaked in kerosene mixed with tobacco juice from his spittoon. He claimed that it kept the mosquitoes away completely and I believe it. Sure kept us away too.

Some of our families had smudge pots smoking by their front and back doors. They'd fill a large can with coals from their kitchen ranges and then stuff green grass on top of them. Somehow, no matter how you tried to place the can, a lot of the white smudge smoke always got in the house and then you'd have to go outside and get bitten until it cleared. When we kids would sleep overnight on a fishing trip up on the headwaters of the Tioga, we'd make smudges too by throwing sawgrass onto our campfire and then when the mosquitoes got too fierce, we'd sit in the smoke for a while. That sure worked but pretty soon our eyes were watering and we were coughing so hard we couldn't stand it. Then we had to suffocate under a blanket, if we had one, or pull our jackets over our heads if we didn't. Those were long nights up there in the bush. Oddly enough, when the trout were really biting, there didn't seem to be many mosquitoes. Probably we were so intent on hooking the fish we just ignored them. One of the best smudges I ever saw was outside a huge hollow pine stub with an Indian in it. He was sitting back in the hole and the smoke was going straight up the bore and never touched him. Pretty slick! I asked him if I could try it for a moment and he grunted "No!"

Many of us kids tried to smoke to keep the mosquitoes away but the only pipes we could afford were corncobs that burned our mouths. Moreover, the Granger or Peerless tobacco we'd steal from our fathers was so strong that we only smoked when we couldn't bear the biting mosquitoes a moment longer. Also, you had to keep puffing almost constantly to keep the skeeters off and that usually made us sick. It was better just to endure. People who have never lived in the U.P. when the mosquitoes are at their peak cannot possibly understand the viciousness of these bugs when they're out in full force. Hardened murderers who escape from the State Penitentiary at Marquette rarely were able to spend more than one night in the woods at fly time without begging at the gates to be let in again.

We joked about our mosquitoes, of course, as we did about all calamities that came our way. Jules LaPorte went around with a sponge tied on the top of his hat, explaining that he'd found a sure fire way to keep the mosquitoes from biting. "Me, I soak dat sponge weeth the blood of a lapin (rabbit) and the flies they go for dat and not for me." He was delighted when a few others fell into the trap and tried it. Another French Canadian with a very bald head claimed that the mosquitoes didn't bother him at all so long as he kept his head bare. "Zee mosquitoes, zey sit on my head and bend their stingers on bone and so can't bite no more." Another man claimed that he solved the problem by putting a bare arm near the inside of a screened window and then, when the mosquitoes poked their stingers through the holes, he'd hit them with a hammer and clinch them to the screen. When he got enough of them anchored there, he said, he'd go out to collect them for soup. Better than fish-eye soup, he insisted.

A lot of lies were told about the size and power of our mosquitoes. At Higley's Saloon there were always arguments about which area had the biggest (it was Goochee Swamp) or the strongest. "I had one that went right through a sweater, two flannel shirts and my underwear and dug into me so deep I couldn't pull it out. Had to cut it off with a hacksaw." That kind of thing. Pretty crude stuff, most of it. I could tell you a better yarn - the one our town liar, Slimber, told about the four mosquitoes, big as pigeons, that sat on a maple limb outside his cabin at Mud Lake waiting two weeks for him to have to open the door, but I won't. The truth, the whole truth, and nothing but the truth has always been my motto. The biggest mosquito I ever saw stood only two inches tall in his stocking feet. Of course, if he stood on his head when drilling for paydirt, he was a lot taller but I don't think that should count. My father, the village doctor, was also a truthful man. He told us often about one time when he spent a night up in Thompson's camp at the Boilers so he could be sure to fish for trout in a beaver pond at dawn. "Never saw the mosquitoes so bad in my whole life," he said. "Almost drove me crazy and I knew that by morning there'd be nothing left of me but bones. So I used my brains, opened the cabin door wide so the hordes could come in, then when they were all inside, I ran out slamming the door behind me. Slept on the grass ten feet away and never got another bite."

Speaking of the truth as being stranger than fiction, Norman Bentti who lives on Easy Street once told me that the mosquitoes in Goochee Swamp were so large they had fleas. Orange fleas, he said. Now Norman is a virtuous man and I have never known him to tell even the smidgeon of a lie. He is trustworthy, loyal, helpful, friendly, courteous, kind, obedient, cheerful, thrifty, brave, clean and reverent, but mosquitoes so big they had fleas? Hoping to sustain my faith in his integrity I made a standing offer of five bucks to anyone who could bring me such a mosquito and damned if Denny Visserink didn't! It was a huge critter and sure enough on the back of its head was a little orange speck, a mite, that moved. Maybe it wasn't literally a flea but it was close enough so I paid up, reciting the old rhymes:

"The flea is wee and mercy me,
You cannot tell the he from she,
But she knows well. And so does he"

"Greater fleas have lesser fleas
Upon their backs to bite 'em,
And lesser fleas have lesser fleas
And so ad infinitum."

Norman accepted my apology for doubting him. "They're hard to see, those orange fleas, but you can tell them because they have blue eyes," he said.

People seem to differ not only in their vulnerability to mosquito bites but also in their ability to attract them. Perhaps it's the body odor. I do know that perfume attracts them. We used to mix it with fly dope and when we smeared that on some fishing buddy, the mosquitoes would come from a mile away to nail him while leaving us alone. White or yellow clothing also seems to bring them so we never wore it. (We never had it.) Those sad souls who always get a bump when bitten (we called them swellers) always got more bites than those who don't. We sure liked to associate with them in fly time. But the best of all things that can keep mosquitoes from biting you is to have a companion from Down Below. Or a fat little baby!

SANTA CLAUS DU BOIS

It was the day before the day before Christmas and all of us were merry and full of the holiday spirit except my father. Upon returning from seeing his last patient, he was glum and depressed all through supper. And afterward, he didn't even read the Chicago Tribune; just slumped in the big Morris chair and stared into space. Finally Mother couldn't stand it another moment.

"John, what's the matter? Are you worrying about one of your patients again?"

"Yes, I suppose so," he replied, "but I'm also worrying about Santa Claus." He grinned at her astonishment.

"I've just been down to see Henri Picotte," he explained. "He's the logger who had that bad compound fracture of the leg when the leaning tree he was cutting sprang back on him as it fell. They call those trees widow makers and they're always dangerous. Anyway, it was a nasty double fracture with a piece of bone coming right through the flesh. I've had him flat on his back in a cast for more than a month now and, although I'm pretty sure the bones are knitting, the wound isn't healing. Ulcerating - a lot of proud flesh and some oozing pus on the wet dressing every day. Oh, it's better than it was two weeks ago but I don't like the looks of it. I keep wondering what else I might do. Henri's a fine big man and a proud one. Keeps telling me he'll pay me as soon as he can get back to logging again. Of course, I told him to forget it, that he could pay me any time, but it bothers him."

"You said you were worrying about Santa Claus, too," Mother interrupted.

"Oh, yes, that too," said Dad. "While I was down there seeing Henri, I heard his wife Marie explaining to the two children that there wasn't any Santa Claus and that there wouldn't be any presents this year. Henri heard it too and tears went down his face. It's hell to see a strong man cry. 'Fix me up, Doc. Fix me up soon as you can,' he said."

Mother had tears in her eyes too when Dad fell silent but she was thinking hard. "We've got to do something for those children, John," she exclaimed. "How old are they?"

"Let's see. I think it was five years ago that I delivered Pierre, the boy. Florette, the girl, must now be about three. Nice kids."

"I'm sure I can get up a bag of toys and some candy from Flinn's store for them." Mother was full of the Christmas spirit. "You can take them down to the Picottes tomorrow when you make your calls."

Dad thought a moment. "No," he said. "I told you Henri is a proud man. He'd resent it. He feels too much in debt to me as it is. That's why I wish there really was a Santa Claus."

The next morning at breakfast Mother was radiant. "John," she said, "I think I've found a way to help those Picotte children have a good Christmas. Let's hire somebody to play Santa Claus and take them the presents I'll put together. Henri wouldn't have to know who sent them."

Dad was intrigued by the thought. "Yeah," he said. "That might work out. But who would we get to play Santa Claus and where would we find an outfit? There isn't a Santa Claus costume or beard in the whole town..." Then he began to laugh. "Just thought of someone who could play the part," he explained. "Old Du Bois could. He's got the white beard and he's short and fat. But that old bugger is the worst scoundrel in town. In his youth he sired half the illegitimate babies in this village and he's spent more nights in our jail for fighting and drunkeness than anyone else. And he's not much better now either. Still drinks like a fish when he can get his paws on a little money. No. Du Bois playing Santa? Gad!" Dad laughed hard again at the thought. He was still chuckling as he went out to hitch old Billy to the cutter.

But Mother was not to be discouraged. She wrote a note and asked me to deliver it to Mr. Du Bois. When I knocked and he told me to come in, I found him eating potatoes and salt pork from a skillet on the table. He really did look a little like Santa Claus, sitting there with his red flannel underwear tucked into his pants, and with a bushy white beard on top of a fat beer belly. "Wot you want wiz me, garcon?" he roared.

I explained and gave him the note. He read it word by word, tracing each one with his fork, until finally he understood. Then he laughed. Oh, how he laughed, sounding and looking more like Santa Claus every minute.

"Your mere, she wan' me be Santa Claus for ze Picotte kids, oui? Sacre mo Gee! An' she pay me ten dollaire for dat? Ho, Ho, Ho! For ten dollaire, I bit ze nuts off a bear, I got so beeg a thirst. You tell her I do eet. I come up see her zis afternoon. Du Bois Santa Claus, Ho, Ho, Ho!"

Oh how my mother scurried around after I brought her back the message. She went up to Flinn's store and brought back a lot of candy and boxes of animal crackers, a doll, and a little red wagon. Then she went up to our attic and came down with some of our old toys. All of these she wrapped with Christmas paper and put in a burlap bag I got from the barn. She also wrapped one of Dad's undertaker cigars for

Mr. Picotte and a box of chocolates for his wife.

"Does he really look like Santa Claus?" she asked me. I said that he really did except for a big brown smear on his white beard at the corner of his mouth, probably from chewing tobacco. I told her about the red underwear and how his belly shook when he laughed.

"Oh, but he can't go out in this weather in that red underwear," Mother said. "Ah, I know. I'll give him that old red deer-hunting coat of father's. I'm giving him a new one for Christmas anyway, the old one was so ragged. But what can we do about a cap? I've only seen Mr. Du Bois a few times and all he ever wore was a disreputable old hat. Let me think."

"How about my red stocking cap?" I asked. "It stretches."

"That's it!" she replied. "We 'll give Mr. Du Bois a new hat and coat as well as money for playing Santa. Now let me put some red ribbon on that burlap bag."

When Dad got home that noon and Mother told him what she'd done, he was pretty dubious. It wasn't that he was afraid that the Picottes would resent the gifts coming from Du Bois but rather that he would probably steal some of them, or take the ten dollars and head straight for the saloon. "You don't know these drunks," he told my mother. "Maybe you ought to give him the money only after he's done the job. Also, ten dollars is too much. Five would be plenty."

Mother was glad that my father was still making calls when Du Bois showed up late in the afternoon. With that old hat and a fleabitten old bearskin coat, he just looked like a bum and a dirty old bum at that. However, once she had him put on Dad's red hunting coat and my stocking cap, he did look a bit more like Santa Claus should. Mother then told Du Bois how he should act.

"You are to knock on the door and say 'Ho, Ho, Ho, here comes Santa Claus' and then you go in and sit on a chair and invite the children to sit on your lap as you take the presents out of your bag. And give them those candy canes first, then the other packages. I have them all labeled. And keep saying Merry Christmas and laughing a lot. Here's your ten dollars and you can keep the red hunting coat and stocking cap. So, Merry Christmas to you and make those children believe in Santa Claus, Mr. Du Bois."

Du Bois felt like a fool going down our hill street in that get up and carrying his old coat and hat as well as the red ribboned burlap bag. He soundly cursed some kids who began to follow him chanting, "Lookit! Lookit! There's Santy Claus. Naw, that's old Du Bois."

He was relieved when he got back to his cabin. There he opened the bag to look at the contents. Maybe there'd be something worth stealing. He felt each of the gaily wrapped packages but they were probably just kids toys so he didn't open them. Indeed, the only thing he took were two of the four bags of candy. After all, he was about out of sugar for his coffee and they'd do in a pinch or he could just suck on one now and then to get the bad taste of rotgut whiskey out of his mouth. Du Bois rubbed his hands with anticipation. After he took those presents to the Picotte kids, he'd head straight for Higley's Saloon and really get polluted. Putting one of the stolen peppermints in his mouth to ease his parched throat, he walked over to the Picotte's house, glad that it was too dark to have anyone see him making a fool of himself.

Outside the door, he rehearsed his opening lines until he had them right. When he knocked and it was opened, he found a very surprised mother and two delighted children. "Santa Claus! Santa Claus!" the kids screamed. They flung themselves on him, grabbing his legs and asking to be picked up and hugged. Du Bois had originally intended just to dump out the stuff in his bag on the floor and leave immediately but he sat down on a chair with a child on each knee and started distributing the presents while Mrs. Picotte went into the bedroom to tell her husband what was happening.

"An' here one for you, little girl and one for you, boy. Ho, ho, ho! See wat Santa he bring you. Open up! Merry Christmas, open up!" First there was a doll for Florette and some jackstraws for Pierre, then a pretty red hair ribbon for the girl and a box of alphabet blocks for the boy. The children hugged Santa and tried to kiss his whiskers, then rushed into the bedroom to show their father what they had gotten. "Merry Christmas! Merry Christmas! Ho! Ho! Ho!" Du Bois was really enjoying himself.

"An here, Madame, I find something for you. Open up!" It was the box of chocolates. Santa got one too as little fingers put it through the white whiskers into his mouth.

"An' for votre pere, too, we 'ave someting, oui! You take it to 'im and tell me wot it is, eh?" he told the children.

"It's a cigar, a big cigar," the boy said when he returned. "My father, he says thank you very much, Santa Claus, and he say to tell you he was almost out of Peerless for his pipe."

There were other packages with more hugging and kissing. Then finally, at the bottom of the sack, were two bags of assorted candies. Du Bois felt a twinge of guilt, thinking of the two other bags he'd stolen but then he remembered the two candy canes he had in the pockets of my Dad's hunting coat and gave them to the kids. Somehow, he hated to leave when he had to go. He couldn't remember a time when he had felt so warm and happy.

"Ho, ho, ho! It's time to go," he roared. "A Merry Christmas to all of you and bon nuit!" Then, picking up his empty sack, he went out into the night.

Two days after Christmas, Father Hassel, our Catholic priest, came up to play another game of chess with my father and as usual we kids had to clear out. Mother told me to haul in a load of kindling and wood for the breakfast fire but then I went upstairs to listen through the register to the men talking. Most of it was chess talk and it was evident that my father was taking a licking for a change.

"Well, Father Hassel," my dad said. "It looks like you've got me on the run. Two moves to checkmate. Okay, I resign."

"A miracle!" the priest exclaimed. "A miracle!"

"Oh, don't go raising your eyes to heaven, you old devil," Dad replied "You know you sucked me in to taking that Queen's Bishop's pawn. No miracle that; just my damned stupidity. Trouble is, that you look so damned saintly I forgot your cunning. No matter, let's have another glass of whiskey. There'll be another day."

"I never argue with an agnostic, Doctor. About three fingers, please, if you will. But speaking of miracles, you and your family performed one last Christmas Eve."

Dad was puzzled. "What do you mean?" he asked.

"Well, it probably won't last," the priest said, "but yesterday Du Bois came to confession for the first time in forty years and he sure had plenty to confess. He told me your wife had hired him to play Santa Claus to the Picotte kids and that he had stolen some of the candy that was theirs and came to realize how rotten he was. He even gave me ten dollars for the poor box. Merry Christmas, Doctor, you old agnostic, you old fraud!"

THE MINER

Ever since he was a tiny lad Tim Trevarthen had wanted to grow up to be a miner. Mine talk had always been part of his daily life because his grandfather who had come from Cornwall, and his father were both hard rock miners. The old man had died but Tim could still remember the gory stories he used to tell, the tales of hair breath escapes when the timber of the tunnels gave way, the frantic climbing of ladders when the hanging wall of the stope let go, the heroic deeds done in the bowels of the earth. The deep tone of the mine whistle at six o'clock morning and evening, the muffled blasts that sometimes shook the earth, the roar of the crusher, these had formed the pattern of Tim's days. And at night, as he lay abed, Tim could hear the ore trains thudding and clanking, and blowing their whistles as they rounded the curve before being switched to the main line that led to the oredocks at Marquette on Lake Superior.

Every morning when we arose in Tioga, we checked the wind. If it was strong and came from the southwest bringing with it not only black smoke from the tall stack, but also clouds of dust from the crusher, all of us closed the windcws and shut the doors tight. There would be no hanging of clothes on such days because they'd be covered in an instant with the blue particles of the specular hematite for which the Tioga mine was famous. It was choice ore, in great demand from the smelting furnaces of Gary, Indiana, and other places down below because, when mixed with ores of lesser grade, it made better iron and steel.

But that dust was sure hard on our mothers. In the winter, it wasn't so bad although our snow-filled yards were colored blue, but in the summertime the ore dust collected in the grass and we tracked it into our houses or shook it off our clothing everywhere we went. At that, it wasn't as bad as the soft red hematite ore that came from other mines, like those that made the Carp River run opaquely red all year around. No amount of boiling and scrubbing could ever get all the red stain from the miner's work clothes that flapped from the clotheslines of those mining locations. We did a little better in Tioga but it was still hard to live with.

Tim didn't mind the dust. As a child, he collected it for the sandpile beneath the big spruce tree where he built little shaft houses over holes in the earth. Heaping up sand to serve as orepiles, he then ran strings over spools to pull up the tin can skips full of the dust. Always he day dreamed that when he was grown up, he would be a hard rock miner too. Sometimes he'd get a chunk of ore that had fallen beside the railroad track and with his father's hammer and a spike, would pretend to drill a hole in it. Then, with some firecrackers saved from the last Fourth of July, he would try to blast off a piece. Once Tim spent a whole day contriving a play carbide lantern out of a tin can and candle, one that he could wear on his cap like the miners did. Yes, when he grew up, he'd be a miner.

But Henry Trevarthen, his father, had other ideas. He'd always made a good living in the mines and now was shift boss on the three lower levels, but he was determined that his son would not also spend his life in the dark depths of the earth as he and his father before him had done. "It's not right for a man to live like a mole or a rat away from the sun," he told Tim. "A miner's work is hard, heavy work. You're nothing but a mule; you're an animal down there underground. Ten or twelve hours a day, six days a week of it and you'll hardly be able to eat, you'll be so tired. Then on Sunday when you might think you could go hunting or fishing in the sun, you'll still be too bushed to do anything but lay around the house like I do."

"And it's dirty, dangerous work, too," he continued. "Miners die young even if they don't get killed on the job, or maimed to be cripples the rest of their lives. I don't know how many a fine big man I've seen all done in. There's always danger around. You keep watching, listening, smelling for it all the time. That's no way to live, lad!"

Tim had heard that sort of thing too all his life but it hadn't made any difference. Whenever he thought he could get away with it, he'd sneak up near the shaft house to watch the huge wheels bringing up the skips full of ore. He liked to watch the little cars shuttling back and forth along the top of the ore pile discharging their ore. He loved the powerful sound of the crusher grinding those big chunks into bits. But most of all, he dreamed about going down, down, down into that mysterious dark hole and making his living like a real man. Tim resented his father's refusal to let him go underground to see what it was like down there as some of his friends had done.

"No!" said his father, whenever he'd asked. "No! If I can help it, the only time you'll go underground is when you're dead. No!"

The conflict came to a focus when Tim graduated from High School. Because he had done very well academically, he gave the Valedictorian's speech. It was entitled "The Rule of Law" and Tim had thought about it for some weeks. He began by saying, "All things are governed by law," dropping a heavy book from the rostrum to startle the audience with the law of gravity, and he ended with a quote from Emerson or somebody saying "To thyself be true!" To Tim this meant becoming a miner, though he didn't say so up there on the platform.

He said it to his father later. "Look, I'm nearly eighteen and it's time to be earning my own living. I'm strong as most men even if I can't handwrestle you down yet. I know you've saved for years to put me through college but I've had my bellyfull of books. If I can't get a job in the mine here I'm going some other place. There's lots of mines in the U.P. I'm set on being a miner and nothing's going to stop me."

Henry Trevarthen didn't say anything for a long time; just held his head in his hands. Finally he spoke. "The curse of the Trevarthens!" he said. "Ay, we're doomed, all of us, to muck out our days in the dark. I ask only one thing of you, Tim. Don't close your mind tight on this. I'll help you get a summer job here in our mine so you can see what it's really like and then in the fall if you'd rather keep working than go to the Michigan College of Mines up in the Copper Country, well I'll say no more. If you were a mining engineer with an education, you'd be close to the mines all your life, but with none of the grubbing and mucking. Well, enough of that." Tim promised to keep his mind open.

True to his word, Henry Trevarthen went to the mining office the next day and explained the situation to Captain Trelawney. "The boy's bright and he'd make a good mining engineer but he's bound he's going to spend his life in the pits. I know it isn't done, but could you fix it so Tim can get a real taste of what it's like to be a miner? He's strong enough to do a man's work, I think. I don't want him abused, but I don't want any special mercy for him either. Let him see what it's like, that's all."

Captain Trelawney agreed. "Just start him on surface, Henry," he said, "and tell the shift boss what you've told me. If Tim's a bloody nuisance, the deal's off, of course. I'll pass the word down about him."

Although it started easy enough, that first month turned brutal before it was over. Tim spent his first week in the big stone machine shop building where one of the two huge horizontal steam engines that ran the generator was being overhauled. The work wasn't hard but it was often very dirty. He swept and polished and once caught hell from the straw boss because he hadn't filled the grease cups on the governor tight enough. "Get your goddamn hands in so there ain't any air pockets left," he yelled. "Poke it tight! Poke it tight!" As punishment, he gave Tim a day in the coal bunker shoveling coal into the chute and about ten minutes spelling a fireman who had to throw the coal through the furnace door into the firey blast. That was awful. Tim's face burned for days afterwards and his eyes kept watering.

Then for two weeks, Tim unloaded logs, lumber, and lagging from a railroad car, a lot of it very heavy stuff that made his back and arms ache so much he could hardly sleep no matter how tired he was. Next, he spent a week with pick and shovel helping dig a ditch to hold a detour steam line from the boilers to the hoist. His partner there was an old Irish miner named Mick Hanley who'd been transferred to surface when he couldn't hold his own underground any more. Mick taught Tim how to muck. "Slow and easy and never jerk!" he said when Tim almost pooped out after two hours of the hard labor that first day. A small man, the Irishman had a rhythm about his shoveling that Tim admired, but found hard to acquire. "It'll come to you, me boy. It'll come to you. Lift with yer legs." He also told Tim to rub lard in his hands when the blisters broke. Mick's own hands were so calloused he didn't need gloves, but it took a lot of hurting before Tim's hands hardened enough so he could forget them.

It was a good thing he'd had the experience because his next job was shoveling ore that had spilled out of the crusher. He had to put the rock into a heavy wheelbarrow and move it away from the base of the structure where it had built up into a huge mound. Five other men were also on that job and Tim was ashamed to find how many more wheelbarrows of ore they could load and move than he did no matter how hard he tried. Also, his boss kept giving him hell for his slowness. Once one of the other men ran him down with his barrow. "Get out of the way, you son of a gun, and let a man work!" There wasn't any comradeship. No one talked. All he heard was an occasional grunt or curse.

The noise and the dust were almost unbearable on that job. For the first time, Tim began to have doubts about becoming a miner. Often when the noon whistle blew he was almost too tired to open his dinner pail to eat the ham sandwiches his mother had made for him. Just the act of chewing was more hard labor until he learned to drink the cold tea with a lot of sugar in it before starting on the bread. Once he was so tired he lay down on the ground at the noon break, too tired to sit up, until the contempt of the rest of the crew made him do so. And there were times at the end of the day when after he washed up in the dry (the locker room), and changed from working clothes to those he'd come with, it was tough to walk home without having his knees buckle so much he staggered.

Just about the time he thought he'd be stuck at the crusher forever, Tim's father told him to report to the shaft mouth to go underground, that the log butchers building cribbing at the twelfth level needed a helper. Bill Plankey would be there to go with him. The steel cage in which they were to descend was not very large, just enough to hold two men in front, side by side, and two more behind them. It was open in front with only a bar across at waist level and had a V-shaped roof of steel above a heavy cross arm from which huge shackles and pulleys and cable were fastened. Above this cage was another cage of similar design, and it too was then empty. To Tim, the cable that suspended these cages looked very thin, though it was over an inch in diameter. He was very uneasy as he stepped aboard and Bill Plankey folded over the guard bar, but he really had no time to be afraid. Bells began to clang and then suddenly the floor beneath his feet seemed to drop from under them. Down, down they went with flashes of light showing where men were working at other levels. Then Tim felt his feet become heavy again as the cage slowed. He started breathing, but only for a moment. Suddenly the cage stopped, then bounced upward, then fell, and bounced again, before it became still. Bill Plankey was grinning as he unfastened the bar and they walked out into a large lighted room carved out of the rock. "Ah, you'll never forget it, will you, boy? I did it alone the first time and had the creepies all night, I did."

When his ears had stopped ringing and he had caught his breath, Tim could see the other two compartments of the shaft. The one on his left held nothing but some pipes and a stairway, not really a stairway, just ladders. "Them's where you go when you can't go anywhere else," Bill said. "And you goes up fast with the devil pullin' yer shirt tail, you do. I know!"

The other larger compartment of the shaft was empty just then. "That's where the skip runs, where the ore and rock are pulled up." Bill said. "The skips probably down at Level Eleven getting filled. You'll hear it roar up when the bells ring again! Yah, you'll hear it and see it plenty before you're done. And feel it too."

After lighting both their carbide head lamps, he led Tim out of the station room into the drift, an eight foot high and five foot wide tunnel. "Pretty fancy, them lights," Bill said, pointing to an occasional light bulb on the ceiling. "In the old days, all we had was candles and these bulls-eye lanterns."

Following the narrow gauge rails on the floor of the drift, suddenly they entered a huge cavern, or stope. "This was the best pocket of ore we ever find in this here mine," Bill said. "We worked this stope for two year before she give out. Made ten orepiles on surface. They say they've hit a bigger one off the sump but I dunno. I seen the diamond drill cores and they sure look good."

After passing through more of the drift and several smaller stopes, Tim heard men working for the first time."They're pushing up a couple of raises into the ore pocket above," Bill said. "One's the men's raise and the other's the ore chute. The men's raise is the one with the ladder in it. Don't get 'em mixed," These raises were smaller tunnels, only about four feet across, and up and down. They gradually angled upward, and weren't tall enough to stand in upright. The men Tim had heard were timbering the drift at the entrance to the raises, putting up rough supports for its roof. "They hit some soft ore here," Bill explained, "so they've got to crib it. We wouldn't do it in the old days, this being a hard rock mine, but all a man hears now is safety this, safety that. Ah, I guess it's all right. They's been too many a skull broken by a hunk of ore falling." He took Tim up to one of the men by the supports. "Here's yer new helper, Pete. Name's Tim." He left.

Pete looked Tim over up and down, then spat a huge glob of tobacco juice at his feet. "For Kee-rist sakes!" he roared disgustedly. "I ask for a man and they send me this. OK, haul up them four by fours here from the last stope and keep out of our way."

Tim worked three weeks with those log butchers and never heard a half-way kind word. No matter how hard he tried to please them, he couldn't. They gave him the hardest, dirtiest tasks they could devise and cussed him out whether he did them well or not. Once, when he was steadying a big tamarack pillar as Pete was spiking a cross beam to it on the other side, Tim had to cough and the big log shook. Furiously, Pete threw his twenty pound sledge at him, narrowly missing Tim's head. That night Tim told his father about it, not complaining at all, but just asking for advice as to how to handle the situation.

He didn't get any advice. "There's a lot of bastards in this world and you've got to put up with them if you're not the boss," his father said. But a few days later, Tim was shifted to a new job. He became an apprentice trammer, and an older man named Jim Engstrom was his partner. Their job was mainly to shepherd the heavy steel ore carts from the blasting sites to the ore raises, or chutes, down which the ore went to the skip. And then they had to push the carts back again. The job also meant some lifting and shoveling although there were other men too who helped fill the carts, or cars, as they were called. Often there were four or five filled cars joined together in a train waiting for them when Tim and Jim returned from a previous trip to the chute. Sure kept them humping.

Tim's new partner, Jim, however, was fun to be with although the work was terribly hard. He had a lot of old mining stories and mining songs, too. One of them he often sang as they pushed the trams:

"My sweetheart's a mule in the mine.
I drive her with only one line.
On the transom I sit and tobacco I spit.
All over my sweetheart's behind."

He told Tim that in some mines the tram cars were pulled by mules that spent all their lives underground and that he wished the Tioga mine had them too. Altogether, Tim enjoyed the two weeks he spent tramming. Perhaps his father became aware of this for soon Tim had a muck stick in his hand again, following the miners who were cleaning up the ore after the holes had been drilled and the rock blasted away from the head of the raise.

This work was not only hard, but danger was always in the air. It was interesting to see the drillers at work with their new compressed air equipment, boring deep holes into the front face of the rock with their long drills but it was so terribly noisy, Tim's ears rang for hours after he got home. And it was scary to see how casually the miners handled the round sticks of dynamite when they inserted them in the holes and put on the blasting caps. It was even scarier to see the men light the long white ropes of the fuses from around a corner and watch the red ash creep along the fuse before the big bang came and the blast deafened him. Even worse than the concussion was the cloud of dust and fragments that filled the raise almost to its juncture with the drift. Even before it had settled, he had to go in there and start mucking. Hard to breathe because every shovelfull raised the dust again. No wonder most miners died young, their lungs full of the stuff.

There was danger as well as dust in the air. Always there was a chance that one of the rounds of dynamite had not gone off or was a sleeper that might go off late, or that a blasting cap was in the rubble. To watch one of the veteran miners listening intently to the blast, trying to guess whether it was as big as he thought it should have been was frightening in itself. Mucking fresh rock after a blast meant being extra careful too. More than one miner had been blown to hell in a handbasket when his pick or shovel set off a hidden stick that hadn't gone off.

Although by this time, Tim had got hardened to the hard labor, mucking new rock in a tunnel where one could never stand up straight almost killed him. His short handled shovel, his muck stick, sometimes didn't give him enough leverage to lift the heavy chunks over the edge of the tram car. Toward the end of the shift, it got harder and harder as he fatigued, and again, compared to the veteran miners, he felt weak as a baby.

Moreover, the rule was that no chunk of rock bigger than a man could lift was to be put in the tram car. Because Tim could never be sure that he could judge them right, he often did more sledging of the bigger chunks than the other miners did. This too took considerable skill. The older miners seemed to have an uncanny ability to know just where to hit a big chunk and have it split into handling size and they rarely had to hit it more than once. Not so, Tim. Often he'd wear himself out banging away at a rock with that fifty pound sledge only to have a smaller and older man laughingly whop it apart in one blow. Tim just couldn't hold his own and everyone knew it. Somehow their patience was worse than the cussing he'd had from the log butchers. He wasn't a man yet; he was just a kid.

Perhaps it was this realization, or perhaps seeing Jim, his old tram partner who'd been so kind, being hauled out on a makeshift stretcher after a chunk of ore from the ceiling of a stope had cracked his skull like an eggshell, but he wasn't so sure this was the life for him after all. He'd done a lot of thinking about everything, he told his father one night the end of August, and maybe he'd give college a try after all. He'd go to the College of Mines for a year anyway and see if being a mining engineer was for him. Tim's mother wept with joy and relief and his father almost did too.

The next week, Tim took the Duluth, South Shore and Atlantic train for Houghton, carrying a very heavy suitcase. But that evening, looking for Tim's work clothes to wash the next morning, his mother found that they were gone. So were his steel tipped shoes and carbide headlamp.

THANKSGIVING

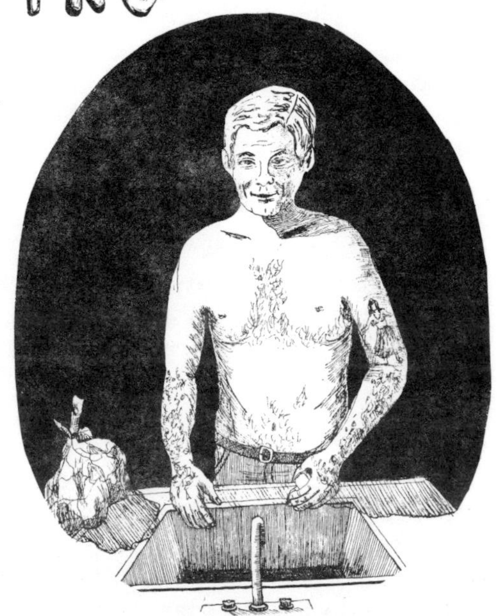

"Come along, Cully," my father ordered. "I'm going to show you how to cut off the head of a chicken. You're eleven years old now and I was doing it at ten." He led me to the chicken yard back of his hospital. In one corner of it was the fattening pen containing two fat roosters that had fed so heavily on corn and table scraps for a month they could hardly crow.

"Now watch me catch one with the grabbing stick," Dad said. The stick was just a long pole with a bent over nail on its end. "You poke the stick out and grab a leg in the space between the nail and the pole and pull him off his feet. Like this." Dad deftly flopped one rooster over on its side and before it could get up, he had the rooster held upside down by the legs. "Now, I'll let it go so you can try it. But first, let's sharpen the axe. You'll find it in the woodshed. And put a pail of water into the trough under the grindstone, Cully. Don't bring the splitting axe. Bring the chopping one."

I turned the crank of the big grinding wheel while my father ground the axe to a fine edge, testing it against his fingernail until he was satisfied it was sharp. Finally, he said, "That's good enough, Cully. Not as sharp as the axes the Finn loggers use, though. Why, they can shave the hairs off their arms with their axes. But this one's all right now for chopping off a chicken's head. Go get me the bigger rooster and bring it to the chopping block over here."

I had some trouble getting it. Not so much in using the grabbing stick as in getting ahold of its thrashing legs once it was flopped over. It beat me pretty good with its wings before I had it under control and handed it to my father. He laid the big bird on the block and with one swift stroke, chopped the head off cleanly, then threw the rooster on the ground where it ran around grotesquely until it collapsed. "Just reflex action," Dad said. "It's good to have it run around like that and get the blood out of the carcass. That's a fine fat rooster. With the other one we'll have a real Thanksgiving feast. I have to go now, so you chop the other one's head off and bring both of them to your mother to pluck. Oh, one more thing. Cut off the wings at the first joint."

It was hard work but I managed it and was pretty proud when I brought mother the two big fowl. She already had two pails ready and after filling them with very hot water, put the roosters in to soak. "That loosens the feathers," she said.

I didn't hang around once she started pulling off the feathers fearing that she might teach me how to pluck. Besides, the smell of wet chicken feathers isn't too great. Instead, she had me go down to the cellar and get the cranberries we'd picked earlier that fall because they had to be sorted and all the bad ones removed.

I had enjoyed that cranberry picking. We had to walk out on the edge of the bog and it moved up and down under our feet. Sometimes our feet broke through and got wet. The cranberries on their short feathery bushes were easy to pick and the pail filled up fast. They were pretty too, all glossy red, with white sides underneath. No good to eat, though. Too sour. But they were sure fine when cooked for a Thanksgiving or Christmas table.

What a Thanksgiving meal that was! We ate at the big table in the dining room with goblets, silver, the Haviland china, and linen napkins. Besides the chicken and cranberries, there was sage stuffing, gravy with giblets, rutabagas, a huge dish of mashed potatoes, Waldorf salad in crescent dishes, wild strawberry jam for the home-made bread, chow chow, and, of course, both mince and pumpkin pie with cheese. All of us ate until we were glassy eyed with distention. Then we had to clear out so Dad could lie down on the couch in the living room and take a nap as he always did after one of those gigantic meals. I helped with the dishes and was about to go out to play when someone knocked at the back door.

When I opened it, I saw a stranger smiling at me. I knew immediately that he was a tramp because over his shoulder was a stick with a red bandanna bundle at the end of it but I told him to come into the kitchen.

"Ma'am," he said to my mother, "could you spare an old sailor down on his luck a bite to eat? The name's Sam Jones and I'm on my way back to my home port in Boston, Mass."

Mother hesitated only a minute. "Of course. Everyone should have a good meal on Thanksgiving Day, Mr. Jones. While I'm fixing it, why don't you go out to the barn and fill our woodbox. Cully will show you where the split wood is."

Sam Jones was a talking man. All I did was ask him if he had a family somewhere and his tongue never stopped. It was interesting talk, too. "Sonny," he said, "I've got a girl in every port and a port in every girl. The world is full of Joneses and old Sam here has scattered a few of them hisself. As for my home, well, here's my hat and I've lived in it in places like Amsterdam and Zoambanga and Hong Kong. For a sailor, my lad, his ship's his home." He had grabbed up a big load of wood and motioned for me to pile some more on it. He was strong! Didn't even grunt when he carried it in and filled the woodbox to overflowing.

When he saw what Mother had laid out on the table, his eyes popped and his mouth hung open. "Ma'am," he exclaimed. "I never seen so much food in my life. Hungry as I am, not having et anything for two days and that was a half can of pork and beans somewhere in Dakota, I wonder, Ma'am, if I might wash up first? A man gets dirty in them box cars and hobo jungles."

Mother nodded and put a washbasin in the sink. "Here's some soap, Mr. Jones, and there's hot water in the reservoir of the range here. You can use the roller towel on the pantry door. We always wash before we eat, too."

She was a bit shocked though when the sailor took off his shirt and, with a great spluttering and grunting, washed his face, neck and arms. Those arms were really something. Hairy below the elbows, above them were a lot of blue-gray tattoos. One of them was of a girl in a hula skirt. Sam saw me admiring it. "Yea, sonny. Got that tattoo in the South Pacific. Want to see her dance?" he flexed his biceps rhythmically and sure enough, she did dance. Wow! Sure wiggled her hips.

For a man who hadn't eaten in three days, Sam Jones ate slowly, mainly because he kept talking all the time. We were fascinated to hear of the strange exotic places he'd been and of his adventures all over the world. To sit there in the kitchen of a wintry house in an isolated forest village and to listen to tales of the seven seas captivated us. Sam said he'd gone to sea first as a boy of fourteen, a cabin boy on a sailing schooner bound for Spain, but lately he'd been on steamers. The last one, he said, was the worst of the lot with a mean captain and mates, lousy food, and rats as big as his foot that bit him at night. So when they took on cargo at Seattle to go back to the Phillipines, Sam had jumped ship and was working his way across the country to Boston.

"Just wanted to see the country, Ma'am," he said between mouthfulls. "I seen the whole world but never my own land. Them Rocky Mountains sure are big, bigger than those in Australia even." Sam said that someone had stolen his purse shortly after he got ashore and that was why he was riding empty box cars across the country and having to beg for food.

When Sam got to his two kinds of pie, he was breathing hard and pausing once in a while. So I asked him if he'd ever been shipwrecked.

"That I have, sonny. That I have. The worst one was off the coast of Brazil where the Zambezi River enters the sea. Only five of us made it to shore and one died that first night. Jungle it was and full of crocodiles, great big critters looking like big logs with bumps on 'em till they opens their mouths like this." He spread his arms then snapped them shut. "And how they bellered at night. I seen one big she crocodile a-giving birth one afternoon on a sand bar and you never hear such a howling when she pushed out of her belly a whole string of little crocodiles, holding on to each others tails. Terrible noise, it was. Scared me, and old

Sam Jones don't scare easy. No, sir!"

He crammed down the last bit of cheese and asked for another cup of coffee. "Ah, that was a bad time," he remembered. "Lots of snakes too, big around as me leg. And the natives in them parts are cannibals. They club you or shoot you with blowguns. Ever see a blowgun, Sonny?"

I said that I hadn't. "How did you get out of there?" I asked.

"Ah, that's a long tale, me lad. We grabbed one of them Indians when he come ashore with a canoe and had him take us upstream to his village where we find another white man who could talk the lingo. A trapper he was, and a gold miner. Wanted me to go along with him and a native up to the rapids two days paddling upstream 'cause there was gold in the sand there. So I went with the two of them. But when we was one day upstream, some cannibals with bones in their noses caught us when we weren't looking and old Sam was in big trouble." He paused.

"Ma'am," he said. "That there was a fine meal and I've et all I can eat. You wouldn't be having a seegar in the house, would you now?" I ran down to the shelf in the cellarway and brought back one of Dad's undertaker cigars. The sailor smelled it appreciatively, then put it in his coat pocket. He got up from the table.

"But how did you escape, Sam?" I couldn't bear to have him leave.

"Easy it was," he answered. "Them cannibals, they like dark meat only, not white. They killed the Indian with us and sent us back downriver in the canoe. Never did find any gold. Not that time anyway but once in Africa..."

My father was in the kitchen doorway and he was biting his lower lip, like he always did when he was angry.

"Pete! Pete Fant! What the devil are you doing in my kitchen? Heard you were in prison."

"Just begging a bite to eat, Doc. On my way home, Doc. On my way..." The sailor grabbed up his stick and bundle and was out of the back door before you could spit.

"Sailor, hell!" Dad exclaimed when we told him the stories the tramp had recounted. "I'd bet Pete Fant never got any closer to the sea than Green Bay where he probably got that tattoo. A lot of loggers go there to have it done. He's a scoundrel, a bum, a no good! Got a girl pregnant, married her, then left as soon as the baby came to shack up with some Indian squaw up by L'anse. He's a cheat and a liar too. He bamboozled a widow up at Sidnaw out of all the money she had and he's been in jail lots of times. Last I heard, he'd been in a knife fight and had been sent to prison." Dad turned to mother. "Don't you ever let a stranger come in the house again. Good thing I was home." He was mad all over again that evening when he found there was no cold chicken for his supper.

Sure shook me up too, and it wasn't until I looked up the Zambezi River in the encyclopedia and found it was in Africa and that crocodiles laid eggs that I knew I'd beem bamboozled good. Just the same, Sam's coming had sure made a fine Thanksgiving Day and I made a little vow that sometime I'd go to Green Bay and get a hula girl tattooed on my arm so I could make her dance.

WILD FOOD

After the mine closed, the people of Tioga had some very hard times but they managed to eat despite the lack of biting money or any other kind. Sometimes toward the end of winter it was bare survival fare but we always made it somehow. I've been remembering the things we ate all through the year, the wild food that sustained us, not only in hard times, but in the easy ones too.

Meat was basic, of course, and fortunately deer were usually plentiful. Venison roasts, chops, steaks, in season or out, were staples in our diet. If we'd shot an old tough buck, we ground the deer meat into patties for our plates or we beat the hell out of it for our stews. We boiled it, fried it, roasted it, and sometimes fed the last remnants to our hounds. Few of our hunters shot big bucks if they could help it; the young spikehorns or does were much better eating. I ate so much venison when I was a boy I've never cared particularly for it since.

I guess I can say the same for rabbits, too. Some of those big snowshoes could also be pretty tough, especially those from a cedar swamp. After the snows came our rabbits were easier to snare than to shoot because they'd turned white. Often their brown eyes were all you could see before making out their contours in the snow. One year though, their winter change of color betrayed them. We'd had a big early snow, and then, when it turned very warm, we could walk along the south sides of our granite hills and spot them easily against the brown leaves. A lot of rabbits got canned that year.

Usually though, we got most of our rabbits by snaring. All we had to do was to find a well trodden runway, put little fences of twigs along its sides, then fasten a loop of picture wire in the middle of it. Five or six of those snares would almost always yield a rabbit or two overnight. There are old folks in the U.P. who still shudder at the thought of eating one more choked rabbit.

Deer and rabbits provided most of our meat but we ate other animals too. A young bear, shot in berry time or in the fall when it was still fat, could provide fine eating. The meat was very dark, almost black, and tasted like a combination of beef and pork. I liked it but some people didn't, probably because they hadn't dressed it out properly. Bears have to store up a lot of fat to hibernate, sometimes so much you have to parboil a bear steak before frying it.

We also ate groundhogs, beaver, squirrels and muskrat. I never cared much for muskrat. The meat tasted like the muck they stirred up smelled. The others were pretty palatable when you'd sickened of venison. I even ate, or tried to eat, an old porcupine once. Staying up at our old hunting cabin at the time, I worked over that old porky for three days and nights, boiling, baking, roasting and frying it. Never could stick a fork into that tough meat but I finally cut off a small slice and chewed on it for maybe an hour before quitting. I still don't know how it tasted.

Perhaps my trouble was that I killed that porky at the wrong time. I'd come across it and another one between our hunting cabin and the lake while they were mating. The only time I ever saw that happen! How do porcupines mate? Very carefully! And a bit nastily, too, as I found when I watched them do it. First, they touched noses, and then the male urinated on the female. She didn't like that particularly but I suppose he was just marking out his territory, like timber wolves did by urinatng on certain stones atop our hills to mark theirs. Anyway, after the porkies touched noses again, the female lifted her quilled tail high and he came close and sat up on his haunches. Then she backed into him, with nary a quill shed. Yes, porcupines mate very carefully. I'm pretty sure it was the male that I clubbed and tried to eat. It waddled more slowly.

Pete Half Shoes, our resident Ojibway Indian, claimed that you couldn't find any better meat than a haunch of wolf, or coyote, broiled over maple coals. I don't know. He offered me a chunk of it once and I was tempted until I remembered that Old Man Salo's big hound was missing.

Fish, of course, were very plentiful in the old days. Rarely would a week go by in the summer without having at least one meal of brook trout, fried crisp in the pan and garnished with a sprig of parsley or a slice of lemon. I never got tired of them. Even ate the leftovers for breakfast. These were native trout, their flesh firm and pink. Occasionally we'd also have a huge lake trout from Lake Superior and these Mother always baked so we could flake off big mouthfuls from the heavy white bones.

Northern pike were good too but you had to be careful of their forked bones. When we'd get one caught in our throat, we'd swallow a chunk of bread to carry it down our gullets. Early in the spring, even suckers were delicious though later they got soft and tasted muddy. Perch and walleyes always added variety and you didn't have to make your tongue feel around in your mouth for bones before swallowing. Many of our Finn families made fish soup with glazed fish eyes floating on top. I never cared much for it. Our French Canadians often boiled a mess of fish of every variety, even chubs, until the bones were soft, then ground the results up fine and baked them into a loaf. Very good! In the winter we rarely tried to fish through the ice. It was just too cold sitting there even after you'd built up a sweat chopping a hole through two or three feet of blue ice. No, winter was the time for the smoked fish that had been hanging from the ceiling of the summer kitchen, or for the marinated ones from the barrel. Oddly enough,our cats would never eat either. We sure did.

We also had fowl, and not just the extra rooster or broody hen from the chicken coop. Partridge was our main poultry dish, and it was excellent if you had a strip of fat bacon to cover it in the pan for otherwise it was rather dry. We shot a lot of partridge every fall but never tried to shoot them on the wing. Shells were too expensive. We'd walk along a deer trail or old logging road very slowly, looking and listening intently. Partridge weren't as wild then as they are now and they did a lot of clucking before they took off. Even then, if you set off an alarm clock in your pocket or had a good barking dog, they'd fly up onto a nearby limb and sit there, just waiting for you to shoot.

Occasionally, we'd get a spruce hen too. We called them "fool hens" because they sure were dumb, or perhaps just curious. They'd sit on a limb and watch you coming. Sometimes you didn't even have to shoot, just club them if they were within reach. Their meat was very dark and I didn't care much for it. Partridge were much better. One old Frenchman downtown always hung his wild fowl in the barn after they were cleaned, until their heads fell off. "Takes away the gamey taste," he said. Perhaps it did but they sure smelled ripe before he got around to eating them.

During their migrations, we also shot a lot of ducks, mainly mallards, canvas backs and blue winged teal. The teal were the hardest to shoot on the wing but were the most flavorful. Coots or mudhens were miserable eating but the worst of the lot were the mergansers; they tasted like rotten fish. Once, when some of us boys were camping overnight, Mullu shot a sea gull and that was terrible too.

Sieur LaTour told us how to set up a fine meshed fish net on sticks, put chicken scratch feed under it, and then when blackbirds and robins collected to eat the grain, to pull down the holding stake with its rope and catch them. LaTour said he'd never used these bird traps himself but that his grand pere had done it in the old, old days. A lot of work, he said, but they made a good meat pie. Four and twenty blackbirds! It's hard for us now to understand how people ate almost anything when times were hard.

Our major vegetables were potatoes, carrots, cabbage, turnips and rutabagas but there were some years when the crop was small because of a wet spring or early frost. Then our people turned to collecting wild vegetables. They waded the shallow waters of a lake to dig up spatterdock roots to bake; they spaded to get the long roots of dandelions to boil. The pith of burdock roots was good in stews. Cattail roots were best boiled but they could be eaten raw too. Pete Halfshoes told us that his

Ojibway mother used to boil Jack-in-the-pulpit bulbs so Fisheye and I tried them once. When they set our mouths on fire with their hot bitterness and we complained, old Pete said you always had to boil them three times in new water each time. Maybe so! Pete also suggested we try skunk cabbage but we weren't too interested. Most of us never ate any of these except experimentally but they were available and some of our poor families used them when they had to. We took some pride in being able to live off the land.

For greens we had wild lettuce, pursley (a garden weed that's hard to eliminate, hence the saying "mean as pussley"), lamb's quarters, young milkweed pods, wild onions (leeks), fiddlehead ferns and, of course, dandelion greens. Of these, I liked the fiddleheads best. You had to pick them in the spring of the year when the fronds were just beginning to unfold. They looked like clenched little green fists, when fresh, but after being canned, they turned darker. The Finns called them *kuolema goru* (the hands of death). Our French Canadians canned a lot of fiddleheads and ate them all winter. A lot better than spinach, they were.

Somehow, when spring came, all of us hungered for green things, not only for our souls but also for our mouths. We chewed cuds of wintergreen leaves; we munched soursap, an acidic sorrel. We'd nibble the succulent bottom ends of timothy hay and wild oats after pulling them from their virginal sheaths. But best of all were wild red raspberry "tucks." These early shoots, when peeled of their fuzzy surface skin and dipped in a bit of salt, sure seemed to fill a basic need and we ate yards of them. Probably needed the vitamins they provided. Perhaps that same need also explains why we would often slice a raw potato and eat it with salt at break-up time or swipe a bit of sugar to put on the first green stalks of rhubarb. There were no salads in our houses when the snows were deep, nor for that matter, at any other time either. We were mainly meat and potato folk.

Most of us had sugar because it was fairly cheap. If you ran out, you could always borrow a cup from your neighbor provided that you returned it with a heap on. But our huge maple trees provided a bounty of sweet sap every spring that, when boiled down, would yield syrup, maple sugar, and maple wax. The latter was a very chewy delicacy created by throwing a ladle of thick hot syrup on clean snow. Sometimes maple wax glued your teeth together but it sure tasted good. We also sucked sap icicles when it froze overnight in sap time.

Occasionally, someone would find a honey tree by sighting the paths of bees as they went home. I never was successful though I sure tried hard and often got stung for my pains. I'd get a can and put it over a bumblebee on a dandelion or some other flower, wait a bit, then release it and try to see which way it went, then can another one and look again. Unfortunately, a lot of them got mad buzzing under the can and nailed me when I lifted it off. I did find a honeycomb of sorts in our garden once but the bees found me so thoroughly too that I never got any honey out of it.

Pierre Moreau got honey every year and Fisheye and I watched him do it one winter day when the temperature was way below zero. He'd spotted the tree and blazed it the summer before so he knew where to find it. As Pierre sawed it down, we could hear bees buzzing around inside and we kept away, much to Pierre's amusement. Finally, when the tree was down, the bees died immediately in the frigid air. Sometimes they popped. Pierre made another cut, then slabbed off a huge chunk to reveal a long comb along its hollow. He gave us each a piece full of honey and grubs and dead bees but I knew my mother wouldn't be interested so I threw mine away before getting home. Tasted like honey all right, but it took three days before my face and hands stopped feeling sticky.

We also ate mushrooms and nuts that we gathered in the woods. Morels, those wonderful wrinkled brown soldiers standing to attention in the spring woods, were hard to find but easy to eat when fried by themselves or better yet when used to smother a steak. We carefully guarded the places where we found our morels, making sure that no one else was following us, because they usually popped up in the same vicinity every year. The other mushroom that was commonly eaten was the white oyster mushroom. It appeared on dead logs a couple of times each summer, usually after a wet spell. Oyster mushrooms arranged themselves in layers on the log and you had to get them early or the insects and deer would eat them. We also ate the fairy ring mushrooms that came up in our pastures at night. All of these mushrooms were dried for winter soups and stews by threading them on fishline hung from the tops of our window for a week or more.

There were few nuts in the U.P. It was just too cold for such trees to grow there but, like the red squirrels and chipmunks, we sure stored up a lot of hazel nuts. They were small nuts, about the size of a fingernail, and they came in a greenish brown husk full of prickers that inserted themselves into the hands that picked them. We'd soak a burlap bag full of hazelnuts in the creek, bang it repeatedly on the ground to thresh them of their husks,then pick them out to put in mason jars for the winter. Or we'd crack them with our teeth to eat them on the spot. Hazelnuts got better as they aged, and on many a winter night, we munched upon hazelnuts by kerosene light until it was time to go to bed.

As I recall, my life as a boy in the U.P. at the turn of the century, I was always nibbling something. In the spring, I ate the little bulbs of spring beauty flowers, or violet leaves. In the summer, I munched on thistle shoots or young burdock stems. In the fall, I chewed wild rose hips, thornapples, wild rice and cranberries. Indeed, we sampled almost anything that grew. Once I dug up what I thought were ginseng roots and was sick for three days after eating them.. If there were nothing better, I chewed maple twigs or straw or spruce gum. It took a lot of unpleasant work to get that spruce gum so it was free from pitch after we had scraped the globs of resin off the trees. Spruce gum was a grayish-pink in color but it chewed good. Sure made you spit!

For fruit, we had apples and berries. Many of our houses had old gnarled apple trees behind them, usually of the Dutchess or Yellow

Transparent variety. They bore heavily every other year but always provided enough green apples for our bellyaches. Every dirt cellar in Tioga had many cans of applesauce on its shelves and also some boxes or barrels of eating apples, especially the Greenings which wouldn't begin to rot until March month. Also, up around the mine and in many little abandoned pastures, we could find a wild apple tree with good fruit. Most of the apples from these wild trees were poor eating without much flavor and only the deer fed from them, but there were a few that had excellent apples. I still remember one snow apple tree down by Maler's homestead that every year bore a good crop of bright red apples with streaks of pink threaded through the crisp white flesh. You'd bite into one of those snow apples and the juice would dribble from the corners of your mouth. Back then our apples had no scab or other disease and no one ever had to spray them with poison. We ate them baked, in sauce, in pies, or just in hand.

But our major fruit consisted of berries. Wild strawberries, red raspberries, blackberries, dewberries, thimble berries, blueberries, we picked them all in huge amounts each summer and they served as our desserts all winter. First in the season came the wild strawberries. Rarely could we pick enough to use them in pies or shortcake. They were mainly for jam or jelly. I remember that once my father insisted that no wild strawberry jam be served when a visitor from a city down below came to our table. "No one who's never picked a wild strawberry deserves to eat that jam," he said. Spread upon buttered home-made bread, fresh from the oven and washed down with cold milk, they were indeed ambrosia.

Unlike wild strawberries, which you picked while appropriately on your knees as if in prayer, our red raspberries could be gathered standing up. We found them everywhere along the edges of the old fields or rockpiles. Some of the best ones appeared along the logging roads a few years after hardwoods had been cut. They weren't hard to pick but you could never really get a heap on your pail of raspberries that would last more than a few minutes because they always settled. With the pails strapped to our belts, we could pick with both hands, the right one for the pail and the left hand for the mouth.

Our women canned hundreds of quarts of red raspberries each year. In season, every house had a little sugar sack fastened to the cupboard above the sink from which the scarlet juice dripped into a pan below so jelly could be made. Oh, those raspberry pies with the red juice coloring the latticed upper crust! My mouth wets with the remembering! Raspberry tarts, hot from the oven, steamed raspberry pudding with hard sauce, or just a dish of newly picked raspberries sprinkled with sugar and swimming in rich cream! Ah, we lived well up in the U.P. in berry time! And I must not forget the warm fruit soup the Finns and Swedes made with milk and eggs and raspberries. Just a bit of nutmeg dusted on top of the bowl was the final touch. I haven't tasted it for sixty-five wasted years.

Thimble berries were a lot bigger than raspberries, although not as flavorful, but your pail filled up fast. Some of us mixed them with rhubarb or apple or both to make a better jam. Gooseberries, once they got thoroughly brown or almost black, were very sweet but the green ones were so sour they'd turn your face into a dead man's skull. Gooseberry jam was excellent on heavily buttered toast and my father preferred gooseberry pie to all others except blackberry.

Anyone picking wild blackberries pays a price in scratched hands and faces or in torn clothing, but they're worth it. I had one special private patch of blackberries that surrounded a deep running spring which I visited every year to bring back the best blackberries known to our parts. Heavy with huge berries, the tall bushes drooped from their weight into the water. I could fill a ten quart pail in a hurry. Then came blackberry pies, blackberry cobbler, and, after straining the juice, the making of blackberry wines or cordials. Our French Canadians always stored up some blackberry juice for the treatment of constipation, but that was made from dewberries, a smaller, ground hugging variety of blackberry.

The great crops of blueberries, however, provided most of the fruit that covered our cellar shelves. We picked them by the gallon, whole families sometimes traveling miles to find the best patches. Every June we explored the plains and granite hills to make sure some late frost had not hurt the little white bells that were their flowers. A failure of the blueberry crop meant that the coming winter would be a deprived one for all of us.

There were two varieties, the blue ones and the black ones, and both could be found either on high bushes or low bushes. The black ones were not as tart or as good for pies but they were always sought after. The people who picked blueberries were of several kinds too: the sitters and the stoopers, and the clean and the unclean pickers. Clean pickers prided themselves on never letting a twig or green berry or stink bug enter their pails and, consequently, they often were slowed down by their persnicketiness. That one little green blueberry seemed to have an almost uncanny ability to bury itself the moment you tried to remove it. My Grampa Gage never bothered. He just stripped the bushes with both hands going at once, much to my grandmother's disgust when she had to clean them on the kitchen table afterwards. "Hell, Nettie," he'd say when she gave him the devil for it, "those green ones give character to the pie, and the twigs and leaves soak up the juice." Most of us were cleaners.

The monstrous tame blueberries of today that come from the grocery stores bear only a faint resemblance to the wild ones of the U.P., at least so far as flavor is concerned, and I will never eat another one. They lack being covered each moring with that Lake Superior dew; their color is comparatively dull; there is no reflection of our clean blue skies on their surfaces. They have no tang. I'd bet even the hungriest U.P. black bear would spurn them if it had a choice.

Our pancakes, muffins and cakes with wild blueberries sprinkled through their batter seemed to shorten our winters because they tasted of summertime. But, oh, those blueberry pies! I've never been able to decide whether blueberry pie is better hot or cold. With a piece of yellow cheese to restore the tastebuds of your tongue and palate to a new virginity after each bite or two, you'd always want more.

After the first fall frost, we'd find a lot of drunken robins staggering around under the chokecherry bushes. Before that time, chokecherries can pucker up your mouth so much you can't whistle, but not after they've been frozen and have started fermenting. Chokecherry wine is very good, much better than that we made of our black wild cherries or dandelions.

Enough! Surely by now you know that we managed to eat pretty well in the U.P. without spending any money. No wonder our kids come back from Detroit when times get hard down below! No wonder we lived long and triumphantly in that hard, but lovely land without vitamin pills! No wonder we had *sisu*!

P.S. *If you want my recipe for sugarplum pie, let me know.*

MUSTAMAYA

It was after supper and four or five men were belly-up to the bar in Higley's Saloon telling their fishing lies as usual. "You know that deep hole just below the Narrows?" one of them asked. "Well, I caught a twenty-one incher there yesterday. A sloib! Never caught a bigger brook trout."

"Aw hell, I caught one that went twenty-two in the Spruce River once," said another. "A big old spawner she was. You ought to see the eggs come out of her. Mighty nigh a pint of 'em."

Higley, the saloon keeper, couldn't stand it another minute. He smote the top of the polished bar with a mighty fist. "You're just a bunch of bloody liars." he roared. "I bet not a one of you ever caught a trout you had to cut to put in the frying pan."

The men were stunned. The unwritten law was that no matter how outrageous the fishing lie, you always nodded your head and then tried to tell a bigger one.

Higley was hotted up. "By God," he said. "I'm sick and tired of hearing all them fish lies. Tell you what I'll do. Any man that brings me a trout bigger than nineteen inches, I give him a ten dollar gold-piece and keep the fish." He went to the back room and brought back a heavy leather purse. "And here's the goldpiece. I'll glue it to the underside of the glass cigar counter so you can see it every time you come here. So put up or shut up!"

As you can imagine, news of Higley's offer swept through town like wildfire and the Tioga River and its tributaries sure caught hell. Most of us had never seen a ten dollar goldpiece. A lot of money, those days. Higley's business sure boomed, so many came to look at it. "Yeah, he assured them. "You catch me a trout bigger than nineteen inches and the gold piece is yours. But no dynamiting! If the eyes are popped out and its bladder busted, that don't count." Higley knew us.

The thing was, we all knew where there was a trout big enough to win that goldpiece. It was Mustamaya, a huge hen trout that lived under the bank of the Tioga in the Pine Pool not half a mile from town. Many had seen her fleetingly and all of us had angled for her in vain. A monster trout. We knew it was a female because we'd seen her spawning at the head of the pool. How did she get that name? Well, "Mustamaya" is the Finn word for Queen of Spades and she sure looked black in the water.

The reason nobody could catch Mustamaya was that most of the time she stayed out of sight, feeding in the deep fast current that had undermined the south bank of Pine Pool. The water ran so fast under the bank there that you just couldn't get your bait to her. It would be swept downstream in an instant. Besides, there were hidden snags down there to grab any hook that had a huge sinker tied above it.

Mustamaya was smart too, for a fish. She'd seen a thousand nightcrawlers and spoons go flashing by and probably preferred minnows or small trout anyway. Some of us had occasionally seen Mustamaya chase a school of those minnows out into the open pool, grab one and swirl back to safety under the river bank. No one doubted that she was big enough to merit the prize. When they looked at that goldpiece under the glass of the cigar counter, they dreamed of Mustamaya.

Slimber Jim Vester, our town liar, didn't even try for Mustamaya at first. Just sat on the bank watching all the others trying to catch her and kidding them when they always failed. When Pete Fouchon waded up to his neck trying to poke his pole under the bank, and had to swim for it, old Slimber nigh to died from laughing so hard. When LaFontaine drove a big stake into the bottom of the pool above the swift run and tethered a heavy line with a five inch sucker on it so it would go under the bank, waited an hour, saw the line vibrate and waded in to haul out a five foot snag, Slimber said, "Damme! Mustamaya's so old she'd got petrified. Why don't you ask Higley to mount that snag over the bar?" Slimber wasn't there when Eino Rutilla fished all night on the theory that big fish fed then but he sure razzed Eino about it. Watching all those fools trying to sneak up on Mustamaya was good as a show, Slimber said.

I liked to go sit with him, watching the chunks of white foam from the rapids above ride down the fast current and disappear under the bank beneath us. Slimber liked any audience, even me. He sure told some good ones. They'd begin nice and easy and believable but then always ended with something outrageous. It wasn't that he varnished the truth. It was the lie that he varnished and polished. You almost had to believe Slimber, he looked so sincere and saintly with his white hair and whiskers.

I misremember most of the tales he told me there on the river bank but the one about the bullfrog comes to mind. We were sitting there in the sun half watching Sven Olson drowning a worm and dreaming of that goldpiece when I said, "Hey, that's a pretty big frog down there at the water's edge. He'd better be careful or old Mustamaya will swallow him."

"Hell, boy," Slimber said. "That's only half a gulp for Mustamaya. Way too small! What I ought to have is that big bullfrog I tamed the summer I spent in a shack at Mud Lake where I crossed that heron with a duck. Named that frog Oscar, I did, and he'd eat bits of meat outa my hand. Great big old bullfrog, he was, maybe a foot tall sitting. You never hear such a croak as Oscar had. More like a boom. Sounded like a man beating on a bass drum, it did."

"How did you tame Oscar?" I asked.

"Twasn't easy," Slimber replied. "Couldn't get to him in the water, of course, but up on land he was almost helpless because he never had learned to jump. He'd just waddle, kind of. Oscar felt real bad he could not jump. Once I seen tears in his eyes when a little green grass frog goes hopping by him." Slimber took a long time filling and lighting his corncob pipe.

"But how could you teach a frog to jump?" I didn't believe him, Slimber being the town liar, but I had to see what he had to say.

"Well, I felt sorry for the critter," Slimber said. "So, I cotched him and put him in a box for a week or so, feeding and stroking him, and giving him a bath with a bucket of water now and then to keep 'im from a-drying out."

"But jumping? How'd you teach Oscar to jump?"

"Don't hurry me, boy. I'm a-coming to that," said Slimber. "After he was gentled, I took Oscar out of the box and squatted down just like he did and then jumped leap-frog way two or three times. Felt like a fool doing it but there wasn't no one around. I could see the big bullfrog a-looking at me, interested like, so I did it again. Then I pushed him down on his haunches and heaved him in the air like in jumping. I done that two or three times but the bugger still wouldn't jump. So I gets me one of them heron feathers and jabs it up his hind end. Goosed him good, and that worked. That old bullfrog, he took off like a grasshopper, a real good jump, maybe four feet high and ten feet long. Then I put Oscar back in the box to think it over.'

Slimber liked the way I was listening. "Was that all you had to do?" I asked. "Just show him and goose him?"

"Well, no. And it wasn't easy as it sounds. Took Oscar a long time afore he'd jump without goosing. Once that heron feather got stuck up his hind end and Great Balls of Fire, he come back to me after the jump with the feather in his mouth - like a spaniel bringing back a duck."

"Another thing too," the old man continued. "Even after he learned to jump good, the critter never really used it for hopping, like a decent frog should. He'd still waddle clumsy-like. Jumping was something special, show-off stuff, and he never learned how to jump down off anything. Oh, he could sure jump up, though. Why, time after time, I'd have to get me a ladder to get him off the roof of my shack. No, Oscar never figgered out how to jump down. Became a real trouble after a time, he did. Once I come near breaking my neck getting that old bullfrog down from a forty foot birch tree, so I heaved him in the lake, hoping to get rid of him. Nope, next morning there he was in his box a-croaking for meat. And he'd boom at night too, spoiling my sleep. Damned nuisance. Even thought of shooting him but couldn't bring myself to do it. Glad I didn't, too, for Oscar, he took care of it hisself."

Slimber knocked out his corncob on a log and carefully filled it with Peerless smoking tobacco from a pouch. Then he tamped it, smelled it, and tamped it again before putting a match to the bowl.

"What happened? What happened, Slimber?" The old liar sure had me trapped.

"Waal," he said. "Old Oscar got better and better at jumping high in the air, even forty, fifty feet or more. He could do it without goosing too but he'd much rather have me do it, than have to jump by his lonesome. Anyway, one night about dark there was this big full moon over the lake when Oscar comes croaking up to me, wanting his bedtime play. Well, I give it to him but used the hot match I'd just lit my pipe with instead of the feather. Wow, did that bullfrog take off over the lake. Way up high until I couldn't see him no more. I never heard a splash and I never see Oscar again."

"What do you think happened?" I asked.

"I *know* what happened, though I can't prove it." Slimber answered. "You just take a look at the man in the moon next time you see it."

I did take that look, and danged if I didn't see a frog there instead of a man's face. You'll see it too,if you look hard.

Maybe it was because I was such a good listener, or maybe it was because we had the straw stack, that I was there when Slimber caught Mustamaya. After about a week or ten days, no one was fishing for the big trout. No one had seen her or even felt her touch the line. They'd given up. Higley's goldpiece would be under the glass of the cigar counter for a hundred years. Oh, it was said that one man tried to sew two fairly large trout together but couldn't do it, and another brought in a thirty-inch lake trout he'd caught in Lake Superior but he'd painted the spots on it so clumsily everybody laughed when he brought it to the saloon. No, Mustamaya was safe and snug in her hideaway under the bank. "She'll die of old age," they said.

Not Slimber! "Now that things have quieted down, I'll catch that trout," he told me. "Ask your pa if I can stir around in his straw stack and catch me a mouse or two? Mustamaya won't touch a worm but she might go for a baby mouse if I can get one." I asked Dad and he said yes, so one afternoon Slimber came up to the house and stirred up the straw. Sure enough, he soon uncovered a mouse nest. The mother mouse scurried away with some little pink mouslings clinging to her teats but several dropped off and these Slimber put into his pocket, stuffing in a red bandanna to keep them from escaping. "Come along, Cully, if you want to," he invited.

I was glad to do so. But first we went to his cabin and Slimber came out carrying a posthole digger and some tackle. On our way down the street we met a couple of men who asked Slimber where he was going to build a fence. "No," Slimber replied. "I'm going fishing. I'm going to catch Mustamaya." Lord, how those men laughed.

But old Slimber knew what he was doing. First, he went down to the water's edge where the current cut under the bank and bounced up and down on the ground until he knew where the solid ground began. Then by squeezing the handles of the posthole diggers, and opening them wide after plunging the scoops into the earth, he soon had a round hole that went right down into the water. We could see and hear it flowing by.

"Now, boy, let's go up on the bank and cut us a government pole," Slimber said. He picked out a straight alder about two inches thick at the butt end and an inch at the top. "That'll do us," he said. "Hell, that pole would hold a horse." Then he attached a very heavy line to the end of it, tied on a hook big enough for a pike, looped a heavy chunk of lead around the line for a sinker, sat down and lit his pipe.

"Well, boy," Slimber said contentedly. "We'll just wait here ten minutes, then I'll tiptoe down to my hole in the ground, put on a mouse and catch that there fish."

And that's exactly what he did. No trouble at all. Slimber waited till the big trout swallowed the mouse, gave a great heave, and there she was, a flopping on the bank. He gave her a good tunk on the head with a stone, put her on a big crotch from a maple branch, and we headed for home. Nothing to it! I felt kind of disappointed.

We only met one person on the way up the hill. Boy, how his eyes bugged when he saw that great fish. "Mustamaya!"he yelled. "Slimber Jim's caught Mustamaya!" Within a half hour everybody in town knew it.

When Slimber Jim got back to his cabin, he put the great fish in a washtub full of water so it wouldn't dry out, had supper, and prepared for a big evening. For once, he'd get respect. And envy! And that ten dollar goldpiece! He measured Mustamaya to be sure. Twenty-one inches and a little over. Nobody ever had caught a bigger trout. They'd be talking about this big one for years, and seeing it too, because Higley had said he'd have it stuffed and put above the bar if anyone could catch one big enough. Yeah, they'd listen to him tonight, they would.

The saloon was full of men when Slimber Jim arrived that evening and pulled the big fish out of his sack. Oh, what a hollering went up when he laid it out on the bar. "Mustamaya! By God, it's Mustamaya for sure. No, that trout's bigger than Mustamaya. Where'd you catch it, Slim? What kinda bait you use? She fight good, Slimber?" The questions and comments filled the air. "Measure it! Measure it, Higley!" they demanded. Yes, it was plenty big enough. Twenty-one, maybe twenty-two inches. A sloib! "Ya got to get that mounted, Higley, like you said. And put 'er up there where we can see it every time we come in this joint." "How about drinks on the house, Higley?"

Without a word, Higley got out his jacknife and scraped the ten dollar goldpiece from under the glass. "If you want to have drinks all around, I'll give you the change," he suggested. But Slimber would have none of that. "You keep the trout," he said, "but I keep the goldpiece! Let them buy their own drinks."

After all the commotion and backslapping died down, someone again asked Slimber how he'd caught the monster. It was his moment of moments but he lit his pipe and took a snort of the whiskey Higley set out for him before he began.

"Well, boys, it was like this. I figgered I wouldn't even try for Mustamaya until you quit thrashing around down there in the Pine Hole. And I figgered, too, that I had to try something different. So I ups and made me this contraption." Slimber laid out on the bar the three foot length of hooks in tandem that he'd put together after supper. The men crowded around to see it.

"Now, all of us know that big trout eat more minnows than worms," Slimber continued, "so I cotched me a little mess of chub minnows and strung them on these here hooks so they'd look like they was a-chasing each other when I pulled the line longside where the river goes under the bank. Every time I seen Mustamaya before, she was chasing minnows. Only thing as would get her out from under that overhang." All the men oh'd and ah'd. Made sense, that!

"How many minnow did she swaller, Slim? a man asked.

"Not a damn one!" Slimber replied. "Twas a good idea but it didn't work. All I did was drown them minnows. Never seen hide or hair of Mustamaya when I was using it."

"Well, how did you catch her then, you old coot? The men sounded mad but old Slimber was serene.

"I done some thinking," he said, "and I come up with the idear that old Mustamaya wasn't going to eat anything as had a hook in it. No, sir! So I gets me an old bucket that had some holes in the bottom to let the water through, filled it with some dead frogs, and anchored it on the bottom with a big rock so when she smelled 'em, she'd poke her nose into the bucket to eat." Slimber filled his pipe and lit it.

The crowd was impatient. "Go on! Go on!" someone shouted.

"Well," said Slimber, "I cut me a good sized government pole and hung a noose from it with wire like we use for snaring rabbits, and I put that loop in front of the opening of the pail so that when Mustamaya poked her nose in to get them frogs I'd give it a big yank and snocker her right up on the bank."

"So you snared Mustamaya? Never hear such a thing!"

"Nope," said Slimber. "She never went near that damned pail."

A groan of complete frustration went up from the crowd. "Quit yer stallin'. How'd you catch her?

Slimber took a long time and he finished his drink before he answered. "Well, boys," he grinned. "If you want the truth, the real truth, so help me God, I got old Mustamaya with a post-hole digger!"

They picked him up and pitched him out of the saloon door and it was only part way open. Higley said later he'd never done such a good business with such a bunch of angry men. Slimber didn't mind it much. He had his ten dollar goldpiece, and for once he'd told the truth, even if they hadn't believed him.

Ten years later, a traveling salesman from Chicago, saw Mustamaya, thoroughly stuffed, and a bit faded, hanging on the wall behind Higley's bar. He'd never heard of Slimber, of course, but what he said was appropriate: "Any man who caught a brook trout that big is a liar!"

LUMBERJACK DAYS

I believe I was about nine years old when I started building a tiny logging dam on the little creek at the far edge of the grove behind my father's hospital. The creek came out of the swamp where the first cowslips (marsh marigolds) always appeared and it dried up in August but in the spring it had a lot of water in it. Like all of us, I had heard many stories of the old logging days when they cut down the white pine forest and floated the great logs down the Tioga River to the sawmill at the edge of the lake. Sitting there, starting to build a dam, that tiny creek was to me a mighty river. I would be a lumberjack and riverman too, opening the dam to carry my stick-logs downstream. Yes, I might even make a little play sawmill with a paddle wheel run by a rubber band, I daydreamed, and maybe even a railroad to haul the boards away.

"Naw, boy, that's no place to put your dam. Put 'er up by that big granite hill." The voice startled me but it was Jim Arnt, an old retired lumberjack with heart trouble, who couldn't do heavy work any more but was able to walk in the woods if he took it slowly. I knew Jim pretty well because my father had commissioned him to make me my first pair of skis and he'd let me watch him do it. Yes, Jim even let me help him lift the rock he used to weigh down the ski after boiling the tip of one end and anchoring it in the ladder to make the curve. He had quite a shop of woodworking tools in his summer kitchen and made cabinets and storm windows and such things. He even had a lathe in that shop, operated by a treadle just like that on my mother's sewing machine. Yes, I knew Jim Arnt and liked him.

"Put 'er up by that big granite hill" he had said, but there wasn't any big granite hill there in the grove. I must have looked puzzled because Jim grinned and pointed to a smooth bald rock at the edge of the little creek downstream from where I had started. It was only about a foot high. Hey, I thought, delightedly, here's a grown-up who knows how to play!

"Yeah, Jim said. "I've helped build three logging dams in my time and I know. Always build them in the narrows between two rock hills if you can 'cause they got to hold back a heap of water if you want to float pine."

"Your first job, Cully," he said, "is to make another channel over here opposite the big hill so we can make a proper dam. Always make half a dam at a time." When I began to do it, he squatted down beside me and showed me we had to begin scooping out the dirt with our hands from the lower end, not the top where the creek was. "Have a hell of a mess if we start upstream" he said. "Once we get the channel cut, then we'll open her up and we can build our dam on dry land."

While I was doing that, Jim got a lot of sticks and notched their ends. "Now, let's build the cribbing for the fill. You put these like you were building a cabin upside down with each big log's crotch fitting into the one below." Again, he showed me, but he sat on the log while I did it and sometimes Jim swallowed a little white pill from a small black bottle he took out of his vest pocket. Once he banged his chest hard. "Damme! he said, "these big logs are too heavy for me now.!" Finally, I had the cribbing done.

"Now, fill 'er up with dirt," Jim ordered and, as I did so, he told me how, when they built Green's Dam on the West Branch of the Tioga, a horse that had been pulling earth in a scoop to make the fill had slipped off the embankment and fallen into some rocks below.

"Right here!" Jim said and pointed to the place where my cribbing joined the rock. "Broke both legs and we had to shoot it. Left it right there. The wolves cleaned it up in just three nights, bones and all. Lots of wolves around that Green's Dam in the old days. We'd hear them a-howling most every night when we were lying in our bunks. Say, come to think of it, Cully, we should have built the logging camp before we started the dam or where would the men be sleeping and eating? Well, no matter. We'll build it later."

That was the first of many delightful times when Jim and I relived the old logging days. I was so entranced by his stories and the things he showed me, I could hardly wait to get out of school to go to the grove. Jim seemed to enjoy it a lot, too.

The next afternoon Jim had gotten to the dam before I did and had spent the morning in his shop building a model of the sluice gate. He was down on his knees fitting it into place when I arrived. It was a little box open on top except for three bars across the opening and two spools with handles on them that acted as windlasses to pull up the gate. This gate slid up and down in side grooves when you turned the spools by the nails driven into the edges. It worked too. "Now you turn this winch, Cully, and I'll turn mine at the same time. That gate must weigh nigh half a ton but maybe we can lift it if we work together." He pretended to grunt with the effort. "Careful now!" he said. "If that handle slips out of your hand, it'll spin fast. Saw a man break an arm that way once."

I held the nail tightly, he made it so real.

Most of the rest of that day was spent building the other half of the dam up to the bypass channel where the water flowed. When, at last we plugged it, we lowered the sluice gate and as we watched the water behind the dam gradually rise, Jim told me more stories of the old days.

"Reason for the dam is to back up a lot of water and let 'er all roar down to carry the logs we'll have to stack at the rollways downstream. Then when the spring flood comes, we'll break out the logs there and let them roll into the river. If we log up above the dam too, we'll have to build some booms to funnel the logs through the sluiceway. Notice, Cully, that there's an apron coming out of the sluice." Jim pointed to a little board platform that did so. "You got to have that apron so the logs coming through won't hit the dead pool just below the sluice but will shoot out down into the current. I've seen some bad log jams, I have, but the worst one was right under Number Two Dam on the Yellow Dog River. They'd built too short an apron and the pine just buried their damn noses in the bottom. Looked like a mountain, that tangle did. Before they could repair the gate so they could lower it, there were logs piled up everywhere and everywhich ways, both below the dam and above it. Took 'em six days with a lot of dynamite before they got the mess undone. You think that apron's long enough, Cully?" He pretended to look worried.

When I tore down to the dam after school the next day, Jim was sitting on a log smoking an old pipe. "I made us a logging camp, Cully. What do you think of it?"

I was delighted. He'd built one out of little logs that was about two feet long and a foot wide. It had only one door but there was a sort of sky light and a little chimney pipe near the middle of the roof. After I had expressed my pleasure, Jim said, "The roof comes off. Look inside." The roof did come off just like the one on my sister's dollhouse. Inside Jim had built two rows of little sleeping bunks along each of the long sides.

"Yeah," he explained, "that's where we slept. No mattresses, just straw, but we were too tired at the end of a day to care. Some camps had two layers of bunks, one above the other, and some slept two men to a bunk, but the smaller logging camps were like this. Silver Jack Driscol ran a camp over by Seney that slept a hundred men, he did. I see you're looking at that bench that runs beside the bunks. That's the deacon's seat, so we called it. That's where we sat. Didn't have any chairs in the camp, though sometimes we'd make a table or two to play cards on and sit on nail kegs there on Sunday, our day off."

He apologized for the tiny stove which he had made from a condensed milk can. "The stove we usually had was a long cast-iron one that would hold four-foot maple logs. It would keep us warm all night after we banked it good. And look, Cully, see those racks hanging down from the inside of the roof above where the stove is. That's where we hung our socks or clothes to dry them out by morning time. Sure stank bad. That's why we opened that skylight to give us some fresh air. Mostly, it was too hot in there if it was closed."

"Didn't you have any windows?" I asked. "Sometimes, but not common," Jim answered. "No need for them. We were up before daylight and in bed by nine o'clock. Nothing to see outside but stumps anyway. Only time we might have missed windows was on Sunday. Those of us who could read - and most couldn't - used the kerosene lamps over there in the corners. And that's where we usually filed our saws and sharpened our axes for the next day's or week's work."

"Where did you eat, Jim?" Don't see any long tables," I asked.

"Oh, not in the sleeping camp," he replied. "We ate in the big cookshack in another building. We'll have to build that some other time."

"I've heard that lumberjacks ate good," I said.

"Sure did in most camps. If a camp had a bum cook, the jacks soon left for a better one. For breakfast: dishpans full of pancakes, sausage, eggs, bread. All you could eat and then some! Noontime, we ate ham sandwiches out in the woods and washed them down with cold tea. Thick, homemade bread sandwiches so big you could hardly get your mouth around the ham in them. Then for supper we'd have meat, usually venison, beans, and potatoes. Turnips, too, with boiled onions and always cake or pie. All you could eat. They fed us good so they could work us hard. Never ate so good since." Jim tapped out his pipe and refilled it.

"One thing though," he said, "there was no talking at meals. You pointed for what you wanted - like butter or sugar. I remember one camp where some newcomer started talking and the cook came after him with a cleaver. Chased him right out of the shack, he did. Cook was king and if you felt like grumbling, you kept it to yourself."

That day Jim helped me build not only the dining shack with its attached kitchen and cook's living quarters, but also some smaller cabins for the camp boss and the scaler's office. Pretty crude, they were, but Jim had brought some shingles so they went up pretty fast.

"What did the scaler do, Jim?" I asked. "How come he had his own cabin?"

"He measures the logs and tallies how many board feet are in them." he replied. "He's the company's man and also keeps the accounts. We had a kind of store, see, where you could sign up for socks or mitts or chewing tobacco, and they'd deduct them from our wages when they come due. Some scalers were crooked, though, and sometimes we didn't get a fair shake. One time the men got so mad they threw the scaler in the river and wouldn't work until they got a new one."

"How about the camp bosses?" I asked. "I heard they had to be pretty tough."

"Tough but fair," Jim replied. "They had to be tough, handling a bunch of rough men like that. For instance, we had one up on the Baraga Plains name of Tom Haskins. Tom drove us hard, he did. Give you a sample how he was like. One of our teamsters, Pete Leary,come back from town one Saturday night with a bottle of red-eye. That's whiskey and no one was supposed ever to have any in camp. Well, we saw him a sucking at it and pretty soon someone had snatched the bottle away and it was passing hand to hand when there in the door was Tom.

Probably heard the commotion and Pete hollering for the bottle. Anyway, Tom seen whose bottle it was and he grabbed Pete and beat the hell out of him even before he got up off the deacon seat. Dragged him to the door and kicked him out of it and told him not to come back. It was blizzarding terrible, it was that night and cold, too, and ten miles from town. Nobody said anything for fear he'd give it to us too, though we knew Pete could freeze to death out there without even a coat on. Pete didn't though. He snuck back and spent the night in the horse barn and come in for his things before we woke up. We seen his tracks. Guess he made it to town. Anyway, he didn't come back. That's how things was, them days. Hard men and hard bosses."

The next afternoon, Jim said it was time to start logging. First, he brought out a compass and we ran a line all around our forty acres of timber. Actually it was only about thirty feet square but he showed me how to spot the corner and then blaze the lines on the trees (Mainly poplar shoots). "You stand here, Cully," he said, "and sight along the compass needle until you find the tree in line with it which I'll blaze. Wave to your right or left until I locate it and then I'll put a slash on its bark. And then we'll change jobs and pace out the boundaries." That was fun and before long we had the tract surveyed.

Then Jim pulled from his pocket a little cross-cut saw he'd made out of a hacksaw blade. It had little handles on it just like a real one.

For almost an hour we cut down those poplar shoots, hollering *"Timberrrrrr!"* every time one was about to fall. The saw made the little bottom cut all right but Jim had to use his jacknife instead of an axe to open up the notch. I sure got the idea about how to fell a tree.

"You should of seen those pines in the old days," Jim said. "Four or five feet across at the butt they were and their tops so far up in the sky you couldn't see it. No underbrush. It was so dark and shady down below it was like being in a church," he said. "A good jack could chop down a tree so accurately it would drive a planted peg right into the ground. Shook the earth when it came down in a crash."

Jim told about some of the lumberjacks he'd known who were extra good sawyers. One of them was so fast, he said, no other man could keep up with him and two men were needed to spell each other on the other end of his saw. And Jim told me of the many accidents when a man got careless or was just unlucky. One of our little poplar shoots was leaning on another and Jim said not to cut it, that it was a widow-maker. "She'll kick back on you and it's hard to know which way it'll kick. And besides, you have to undercut 'em first." "Even with wedges, they're scary to cut," Jim said. Somehow the way Jim described what a falling pine could do to a man was so real I shuddered.

After we'd sawed down ten or twelve of the little poplars, we cut each of them into sticks, all of the same length, and took off any little leaves or branches. "Now, we've got to skid them out to the river road," Jim ordered. "We'll need horses or oxen for that but since we ain't got none, we'll just have to pretend we have. You make the river road first and then the skid trails up to where we've cut the pine." He showed me where to scrape out the road so it would be level. When I'd finished, Jim had carved a little horse out of a chunk of wood but it was time for supper again, so we had to quit for the day.

The next afternoon, we hitched Jim's little wooden horse to each of the logs and hauled them to the river road. "Now, we've got to wait for cold weather," he said. "No, it's already winter and they've had the sprinkler making ice on the river road so let's haul our logs to the rollways below the dam." Then again, from his pocket, Jim brought out another toy tool, a cant hook, made of a stick with a curved wire hinged to its end. He showed me how a man with a cant hook could roll a log, one so big he could not possibly lift it, almost any place he wanted it to go. "With a cant hook or peavey, and a pike pole and an axe, a couple of strong men can make any log behave," he said. I asked him what the difference was between a cant hook and a peavey and he told me they were the same, that a peavey just had a sharp spike in its end.

Our rollways were on a little rise beside the creek bank. Below them we put three of our little logs to act as skids down which the logs could roll into the river when it was time to do so. Jim said that stacking the logs at the rollways (he called it decking) was always dangerous work and that breaking the piles was worse. He told me some harrowing tales about men being killed on these jobs.

I noticed that Jim was having a lot of trouble breathing, especially when he bent over, so I asked him if he were sick. "Naw," the old man answered. "Just the same old thing. My pump ain't what it used to be. Your father he examined me and said I had to take it easy, but old Jim's not bedding himself down yet. Being down here with you, Cully, helps me remember better days and feel good." He sure walked slowly going home.

Jim didn't show up the next afternoon and I sure missed him. The water behind the dam had backed up to form a little pond and soon it would be running over the top so I opened the sluice gate a little. When the flood of water rushed through the opening, I put a few little sticks in above the gate and watched with delight as they went through it and over the apron into the current below. It was time to break the rollways but somehow I couldn't do it without Jim being there so I went down to his house to see how he was.

The old man was in his bed with all his clothes on but he grinned when he saw my worried look. "Just taking the day off, boss," he said. He asked me how the logging operation was doing and I told him how I'd opened the sluice gate and how the logs had floated through fine. "Maybe I'll be feeling better tomorrow," the old man said, "and I'll tell you how us old river hogs used to drive the logs downstream." I was so concerned about Jim that when I got home I asked my father to go see him. Sure looked sick.

Dad wasn't too optimistic when he returned. "I listened to his heart with my stethoscope,", he said, "and there's a lot of arhythmia and skipping beats. I changed his medication to some stronger stuff and maybe that will help, but Jim's got to take it easy and never get excited. A few days in bed may help. I got Mrs. O'Canton to fix him something to eat and to look in on him several times a day. About all I could do."

Jim had reminded me that we hadn't built the horse barns or blacksmith shop so that's what I spent the next few afternoons doing. "Have a hayloft above with a hole to throw the bales down and make a stall on one end for the horses and on the other end for the oxen," he ordered. "Oxen always seem to do a better job of skidding than most horses. They're slow but strong." I did my best to follow his instructions but my barn didn't look as good as the men's cabin or cook shack that Jim had built.

I also cut a lot of other little logs but cheated a bit because I used a hatchet instead of the little cross-cut saw Jim had made for me. I did skid them out to the river road. It was a week before the old man appeared again, this time to bring me a minature logging sleigh he had made. It even had strips of tin to serve as runners and a little yellow chain to hold the logs on it. Looked like a watch chain. Jim said he was feeling much better and knew that it was time to break the rollways. "I see that you've got the sluice gate part way open," he said. "That's good. She's a-building quite a head of water above our dam. Plenty to float the logs, I figure." He also admired my horse barn. Said he couldn't have built a better one himself. That wasn't true, but it made me feel proud anyway. Then he had me haul the logs in the new sleigh with the chain holding them down tight and pile them up along the others on the rollways.

"Well," he said. "Looks like it's about time for the log drive, boss. Get a crew of riverhogs and station them about a quarter mile apart along the river to watch for log jams. OK, break the first rollway!"

When I released them, the logs rolled down the three slanting skids and into the flooding creek. "Thar she goes!" he yelled. "All the way to Lake Tioga. Let her rip! Better open that sluice gate all the way and break another pile." He sure was enjoying himself and so was I.

Suddenly Jim let out the old riverhog's yell: "Ah-ee, Ah-ee. There's a jam a-coming down there at the bend," he shouted. He explained that when the rivermen above or below heard that cry, they passed it along and then came running. A little log jam was indeed forming at the bend and soon the logs were tangled in every direction, even piled up on each other. The water was backing up behind them.

"Got to get the key log out right away, boss," Jim yelled and he ran down with me to the bend. "There she is. That big one there on the angle, with its butt up in the air, is the key log." I tugged at it and when it finally came loose, the log jam unravelled itself and the sticks began to float downstream again, slick as a whistle.

"Boss, we got that just in time," Jim exclaimed. "A few hours more and there'd be logs backed up right to the rollways." He wiped his brow and breathed hard for a time. He'd got too excited, I guess, and he sat on our log for quite a spell saying nothing. Then he began telling stories of logjams and riverhogs in the old days.

"After the cutting was done and the logs were piled up at the rollways," he said, "most of the lumberjacks were laid off. Only ten or fifteen of the best of them, those that had experience driving logs, were kept on. A man was proud to be on those crews. Had to be a good man, one with cat feet, because riding those logs took a lot of jumping from one to another. We'd use our peaveys for balancing or to steady ourselves when we got a good rider log. Of course, we didn't just ride the logs except when we had to go out on them to keep them running straight, but there were times when you sure did and you had to be able to birl a log too."

"What's birling, Jim?" I asked.

"It means making the log turn around under you," he answered. "You jump up in the air and then when you come down, you stomp on it just off center and it'll start turning. You can steer a log some by birling and bring it closer to another log you might want to get on."

"I'd think you'd slip," I said.

"Yeah, and some did and paid a price for it," Jim answered. "Of course, we had corked boots, boots with sharp hobnails in their bottoms, and they helped plenty. We used to file them corks so their points were needle sharp. But even so, running across those fast floating logs was no Sunday School picnic. Never forget how a friend of mine, Jack Manning, slipped and fell between two big logs into the black water and then they rolled together. I can still hear how his skull popped. Never did find the body either! Almost every drive, some jack got killed or crippled but we got the logs down, we sure did. No job for a greenhorn." He was silent a long time remembering.

At last, Jim roused himself and lit his pipe. "Well, that's how it was in the old days, boss," he said. "Tomorrow, we'll start building the sawmill down there by the lake. Time to get back to camp, boss." We walked very slowly back up the path, resting often.

There was no tomorrow. Jim died that night and somehow I never could bring myself to go back to our little dam. Not until last summer, sixty-five years later, when I had a beard whiter than Jim's had ever been. Everything had disappeared except the rock against which we'd built our dam. At the place where our rollways had been, I found a glint of yellow watch chain half buried in the leaves.

GRAMPA REBELS

When a boy reaches the age of ten, he has many needs but the greatest of these is to have an adult male companion to be his hero. My Grampa Gage certainly fulfilled part of that requirement but he was so thoroughly hen-pecked by Grandma, I just couldn't worship him the way I wanted to. At the beginning of this century in the U.P. it was a man's world and any thought of women's lib would have been incomprehensible. Men were inherently superior to women, of course, and so were boys to girls. Rarely did a man and wife walk down the sidewalk together; she followed him. He made the basic decisions - or thought he did. It wasn't that he had any need to prove that he was macho; it was just the way things were, the way they'd been ordained.

That was why I always felt so bad when Grandma constantly humiliated the man I loved. You could see that she enjoyed doing it, ordering him around as though he were her slave, telling him, and everyone else, how stupid he was, bad mouthing him at every opportunity. Grampa wasn't a bit stupid. He'd been a lumberjack and a teamster as a youth before he went to a business college in Detroit to improve himself. Thereafter, he ran a successful grocery store, and then became a banker. Unfortunately, the bank failed when his friend, the cashier, absconded with all the bank's liquid assets and went to South America. Grandma never forgave her husband for the bank failure although he'd had the foresight to put the house in her name along with a considerable amount of his stock holdings. This left her rich and him poor, a situation about which she constantly reminded him with her nasty tongue. In his old age, he even had to ask her for tobacco money, and often went without smoking because he knew she'd give him hell all over again.

I probably should describe my Grandma Gage. She was a formidable looking woman, as tall as Grampa, always well dressed and very proud of her figure which she contained inside a whale bone corset that Grampa had to lace up each morning and unlace each night. Her gray hair was immaculately coiffed in a pompadour with never a strand out of place. When she was angry, which was her usual condition, her jaw stuck out and her blue eyes blazed. A dowager!

Grampa was a slim, wiry man in his late seventies. He gave the impression of having great dignity but there was always the hint of a smile under his grey mustache and the corners of his eyes held memories of much laughter. Away from Grandma, and he stayed away all he could, he was the most joyous, imaginative person I've ever known. He not only knew how to play, but also how to pretend. Every day Grampa and I would assume new roles on our forays into the fields and woods or when we did our various projects. One day, we'd be Indians; another day antelopes, or trees, or beavers making a dam across a little creek. He gave me a new name every morning: Mr. McGillicuddy, Mr. O'hallahan, Julius Caeser or such and he would call me by it all day or else call me "Boy." Grampa, with me, was a little bit crazy, but then so was I. We sure had fun.

The day of Grampa's rebellion started like all of our lovely days together by my watching him shave at 5:30 a.m. As usual, he had managed to give me a noseful of lather despite my watchfulness and was just scraping the first bit of it off his own face when Grandma called from the bedroom. "Arzeee!" she screeched. (His name was Azra T. Gage.) "Fetch me a glass of water!"

"Be with it in a bit," he answered. "I'm shaving."

"Arzee! I want that water right now! Do you hear me? Right now!" Everyone else in the house could hear her, she screamed so loudly, and my little sister, Dorothy, aged three, began to cry in her bed. Grampa sighed, put down his long razor and was filling the glass when Grandma started yelling insults and just raising verbal hell loud enough for the neighbors to hear. And even after he brought her the glass of water, she didn't drink it until she'd laid him out in her usual nasty fashion. How I hated the old she-devil! How could he put up with her? Why didn't he hit her?

I asked him that when he returned to complete his shaving.

"Well, Mister Hoogerhyde," he said. "I, sir, am a man of peace, as your grandmother knows well. There have been times in the forty-seven years since I married her when the temptation to smack her a good one in the kisser came to me but I fought it down, Mr. Hoogerhyde, but I always fought it down. For I am a Gage, sir, and a gentleman, God help me. It's *noblesse oblige,* you see. We Gages come from royalty and the king never slugs the queen. Repeat after me," he ordered. "A Gage and a Gage, and the son of a Gage, a Gage of the royal line. From every rugged feature, ancestral glories shine!"

I said it over and over until I had it memorized but somehow it didn't explain why Grampa always took her abuse so patiently without any protest at all, never fighting back.

That morning, after breakfast, Grampa said he wanted to be an ab-or-iginal pre-his-toric caveman. (He always sounded out the big words for me.) I was Ugo, he said, and he was Bugo and we'd better find us a cave right away before some dinosaur or other varmint got us. Well, the only place that resembled a cave near our town was a narrow passageway between two huge rocks up on Mount Baldy, so I led him up there, being careful to keep a sharp look-out for monsters all the way. We roofed over the space between the rocks and it really seemed like a cave.

"Now, we'd better make some weapons, Ugo!" Grampa commanded and before we were done, we had a stone axe made of a sharp rock bound with his shoelace between the ends of a cleft stick, two spears, and a pile of throwing rocks. That wasn't enough, Bugo said to me. "Homo sap must have fire to be safe!" He sent me out to gather some sticks and when I returned he had a little fire going. "Bugo make fire by twirling sticks," he growled but I knew he'd used the same match with which he'd lit his pipe. Then he ordered me to go out and kill a zebra and bring back a couple of leg bones to eat. When I returned with two knobby hunks of wood he praised me. "Ugo mighty hunter. When Bugo die, Ugo be chief!" We were toasting the wood chunks over the fire and pretending to gnaw them when suddenly Mullu's old hound appeared.

"A saber toothed tiger!" Grampa roared. "Build up the fire. Get your spear!" He sounded so fierce the old hound ran away. "Phew!" Grampa said, wiping his brow. "Ugo, that was a close call!"

But somehow that old flea-bitten hound had shattered our fantasy and we came back to being ourselves again. "Something's bothering you, Boy. What's wrong?" Grampa asked.

I tried to tell him again how awful I felt when he let Grandma constantly insult him and treat him like a dog. I know I was half crying as I explained my need for him as a hero as well as a companion. I didn't ever say hen-pecked but he knew what I meant.

At first, he made a little joke about it, unbuttoning his vest and raising his shirt tail and underwear. "Ah, but you don't understand, Boy, that I have a secret weapon," he said. "When Grandma starts giving me hell, I just press this belly button and I don't hear a word she's saying." But somehow that didn't help at all and we went back to our house silently. It was time for dinner, anyway.

I'll never forget that meal as long as I live. Oh, it started out like every other noon meal with good food and conversation but before we had finished our apple pie, Grandma had completely spoiled it with another of her usual tantrums. She was just poisonous. She told my mother that the pot roast had been overcooked, and that the boiled onions were too hard. She snapped at my five-year old brother, Joe, for trying to talk with food in his mouth. She argued with my father about politics. She told me my hands were still dirty though I had washed them. She insisted that my sister sit up straight in her high chair. But most of all, she concentrated on Grampa's sins of commission and omission, even bringing up the bank failure again. She was just awful. I could see my father biting his lower lip, a sign that he was about to explode, but it was Grampa who did.

I've mercifully forgotten the last humiliating thing she said about him that made him rise from the table and go over to her on the opposite side of the table. "Henrietta!" he roared. "That's enough! I've borne your vicious tongue for forty-seven years. I've suffered your insults and tantrums too long. You have shamed me before my son and grandson too many times to count. But no more, Henrietta, no more! From now on, you will keep a civil tongue in your head, stop nagging me, and be the lady you profess to be, or I shall do to you *anywhere* what I'm going to do to you now!" Very calmly, he grabbed her hair and lifted it from her head and waved it high. We gasped to see that she was bald as an egg. None of us knew that Grandma wore a wig.

Grandma let out a shriek, covered her naked pate with her hands and fled upstairs to her bedroom, sobbing. Grampa knew that it was his finest hour because he ate the rest of his pie very slowly and had an extra piece of cheese. Then he arose, tucked Grandma's wig onto his belt, and motioned me to follow him. I couldn't help hugging his legs, I was so proud of him. We went out to the clothesreel and took turns dancing around it, playing Indian, and waving Grandma's scalp.

She never hen-pecked my hero again.

GOLDEN ANNIVERSARY

"Yah, that was a long time ago, Eino," Hilda said, looking up from her embroidering. "Fifty years ago, 1865." She knew what her husband was thinking about. Lately, the two of them almost always seemed to know. Tomorrow would be Midsummer's Day, their marrying day, their golden anniversary. She had put cedar branches all around the house and hung the green strings of groundpine over the kitchen windows. Eino had got them for her from the swamp so they were fresh and smelled good. He was a good man, Eino was, rough on the outside but tender in. They'd told her a Swede girl should never marry a Finn but they were wrong, fifty years wrong.

Her husband was sitting in the soft chair with his feet on the butter churn looking out of the open window, feeling the soft air blowing through the screen, and watching a few mosquitoes hunting for holes in it. "I was scared getting married," Eino said to her. "Only twenty, I was. Had job but no money and I was shamed to bring you to that shack I built. I got drunk fifty years ago tonight."

Hilda smiled. "Don't say that! We had good times there, Eino; raised babies there. I still miss old cabin sometimes, even though this big house better one. Old cabin always warm. You chink it good with swamp moss, Eino. You always take good care of me."

The old man grinned. "But lotsa mice in old cabin, Hilda, eh?" Hilda could never stand mice. They frightened her. Bears didn't. Like the time she shot a big bear trying to come through the summer kitchen window when she had little kids and he was away. And chased Salo's bull out of her garden! No, Hilda was no coward. Only for mice. He'd been lucky marrying Hilda that Midsummer's Day so long ago, in that new blue serge suit he'd sent the money order for. Didn't fit too good, but he sure felt dressed up there before the Justice of the Peace in Ishpeming. And Hilda in her new outfit too, holding his hand as the words were said. So pretty, she was. Yellow hair,like gold, in tight braids. Eino told her what he'd been remembering.

"Oh, no, Eino," she said. "You had brown suit, not blue. Blue suit you had for christening John and Olga. I know. I help you buy it in Ishpeming at Brastaad's. But you looked handsome in brown, Eino. And so strong. Big muscles." She smiled again, remembering how his hand had trembled in hers. Eino had really been scared that marriage day. He'd always been shy too, but when they got off the trail and started up the hill street, he'd insisted that she walk beside him, not after him like all the Finn women of that time did.

Then she also remembered that first supper in the old cabin. Mrs. Thompson, the woman she'd been the hired girl for, had given her a four-place setting of blue willow ware china for a wedding present, and knives, forks and spoons and a red and white plaid tablecloth, too. Hilda remembered how nice the homemade table looked when they sat down for their first meal together.

Eino turned from the window. He'd been remembering, too. "We had ham and eggs and potatoes," he said. "and coffee cake. Those dishes were best we ever had. Too bad they broken and gone." They'd eaten off them for fifty years, or almost. Maybe two plates and a chipped saucer were left, but the cat had broken the last blue cup only the month before. Somehow, coffee didn't taste as good any more. Those sure had been pretty dishes.

Getting out of his chair, the man groaned a bit. He got a stub of a pencil out of the button box he'd made for Hilda thirty, forty years ago, and began to do some figuring on the back of an old calendar. How many meals had they eaten on those dishes? Three hundred sixty-five times three made 1,095. Then, times 50, make it 54,750, about that. He told her the incredible figure.

"You cook me some 54,000 meals, Hilda," he said. "And all good ones too. You been good wife, Hilda."

"Yah," she answered. "And 54,000 washings of those dishes too. But sometimes you help, Eino. Not like other Finn men. You know when I too tired or sick. And you cook breakfast sometimes so I can sleep late. You good man, Eino. Always been good to me." She got up and put her bare arms around his neck. He always liked that.

Eino patted her hands. She had been a good helper too, Hilda had. He remembered how in the old days when they were very poor, she'd not only helped rake the swamp hay he'd cut with the scythe, but also carried her stick pole of it back up the long hill to the barn. Not as much hay as he could carry, but plenty at that. And hoeing the tough quack grass out of the new potato patch before he got back from the mine. And helping with the butchering of the pigs and steers and deer. And doing all that milking for years and years. Some women were lazy. Not Hilda. Her hands showed how much she had worked for him and the kids, hands that were gnarled and had swollen knuckles. They were beautiful hands. How many washings had they done? He didn't want to count.

Hilda was looking at Eino's hands too as he filled his pipe. She noticed that they trembled when he stuffed in the tobacco and that he couldn't straighten them out all the way any more. Too many years of hard shoveling up at the mine. But they were the hands that had brought her wild flowers, not only in the early years, but even that very day. She looked at the blue flags, the wild iris, in the white pitcher. Eino always knew that they were her favorite and he'd probably gone all the way to that swamp by Mud Lake to get them. Most Finn men never did that sort of thing. Eino liked to see flowers in the house: pink arbutus first thing in the spring, then yellow cowslips and pink lady-slippers, then the blue flags and wild roses. In the summer, daisies and Indian paintbrush, and last in the fall the goldenrod, fireweed and blue asters. Eino had planted lots of them in the front yard by the porch too. Yes, Eino liked flowers as he liked her. Once he had called her his Swede blue gentian - because of her eyes, he'd said. That was why she soon must be starting slips from the old geranium so they could have cans of scarlet in the windows next winter.

As he lit his pipe, Eino glanced at her. "A fine looking woman still," he thought. "Always neat." Hilda sure looked pretty right now in that yellow dress. Not like the dull black and brown dresses most Finn women wore around the house. It was probably the Swede in her but Hilda always wore bright things, reds, and blues and yellows. They helped the winter go by. He'd never tired of looking at her - her braided hair, the way she dressed, the way she moved.

Eino grinned a little ruefully, remembering one other Mid-summer's Day when he'd bought her some yard goods for a dress she could make. He'd known it was a mistake the moment she put eyes on it. She did make herself a skirt out of it and wore it just once because it looked terrible on her. Made her look like a gypsy woman. A color for hearses, that purple. He chuckled aloud.

When she asked him why, Eino told her and she laughed too. But then she reminded him of the mustache cup she'd bought for him one year because she thought he'd like it and wouldn't keep getting coffee stains under his nose when he drank from the blue willow ware cups. That too had been a mistake. Eino had tried valiantly to use that cup because it was a present from her, but he'd hated the damned thing so much he finally shaved off his mustache so he wouldn't have to use it. They both laughed, remembering how little Elsa hardly knew her father without that mustache.

That brought back the memory of Elsa's birthing. It had been a hard one. No doctor that time like she'd had with John. Just an old Finn midwife and the pains were long and fierce. Eino had stayed with her through all of it, holding her hand and squeezing it hard when the pains came. He'd given her the biting stick to sink her teeth in that he'd made out of soft basswood for her when John was born. It really helped, she said, or at least it helped her keep from screaming. She still had that biting stick somewhere among her private treasures.

Eino remembered that labor, too. That's why they'd had no more children. Two of them were plenty anyway. He just wished they lived closer so they could be there for this golden anniversary tomorrow.

Hilda would like that. But John, his son, had a good job in Detroit, a white collar job. He was an engineer. It had been hard helping him get through college, but he'd worked most of his way and managed it somehow. Maybe John could come up later this summer on his vacation and bring the grandsons along. Little Eino was a good fisherman. He'd take him trolling in Lake Tioga for northerns.

Hilda was wishing, too. Elsa was married and expecting her third child so she couldn't come. It would have been a long trip on the train from Traverse City where she lived. Maybe two or three years from now Elsa could come home; she probably needed some babying herself. But, as always, it would cost lots of money and Elsa and her husband didn't have much of it. For that matter, Eino and she had never had much money either.

"Maybe if we had sent John enough for his ticket, he might have come," Eino thought. He and Hilda had talked it over but decided against it. John wouldn't take it anyway. He knew that his father's little mine pension didn't go very far even though they didn't need much except for eating money and the taxes. They had to save some out of each month's check for those taxes that came due in January. Probably he would have to tap Hilda's blue sugar bowl again. Eino smiled, remembering how they'd lived out of that sugar bowl for a month when the mine suddenly closed down. Hard times, back then, until he got a job on a railroad section gang, tamping ties. He'd even quit smoking to save money until one morning there was a can of Peerless on his blue willow ware breakfast plate. Hilda had bought it with her butter and egg money. Yes, Hilda had been a saver. She knew how to buy and keep. He told her so.

"But remember that big fight we had when I told you to take our bank savings and buy those forties?" she asked.

Yes, Eino remembered well. He and Hilda hadn't had many real fights or mean arguments. Oh, of course, there had been little ones, especially when they were first married. She liked her oatmeal soupy; he liked his hard and granular. She liked her bacon with the fat barely cooked; he wanted his bacon brown and crisp but limp. He liked thick pancakes like his mother had always made; Hilda preferred thin ones like those she'd had at home. But those were little arguments and they'd compromised. One of the big fights had been when Eino had been given a chance to go underground in the mine and was thinking about doing it. Paid much better than surface work, but Hilda said a big *No*! When he'd insisted that where a man worked was his decision, she answered that she would leave him if he did, and she meant it. He gave in finally, but got sick-drunk that night at Higley's Saloon, the only time he had done that since he got married. Good thing too that he hadn't gone underground because a week later they had a bad accident down there. Hilda was a smart woman, smarter in some ways than he was.

Hilda was remembering the other big fight. Reino Untilla had offered to sell Eino five forties of freshly cut-over land for three thousand dollars. At that time they had only about four thousand in the bank, their entire life savings. It was for their old age and funeral expenses. Hilda wanted Eino to buy the property. They were only in their thirties, she said. In twenty or thirty more years, there would be another crop of spruce and balsam to be cut and they'd have lots of money for their old age and the kids too. Eino didn't agree. He had no life insurance. The mine might close down again. That raha in the bank had been hard to save and with the kids, it would be harder still. They would have to pay taxes on those forties every year. It would be crazy to buy them.

"No," said Hilda. "It's a good buy. It's our one chance to get a lot of money for our old age and to leave some to our kids. We'll get along. I'll go back to being hired girl if I have to." They argued about it for weeks until Eino finally gave in and reluctantly bought the property after paying five hundred dollars more for a life insurance policy. That deal had been a sore between them for years but finally it had healed. Eino knew now that he was almost a rich man because a jobber had recently offered him three thousand for the stumpage of just one forty. Yes, Hilda had been smart about that timber. Once when he admitted it to a friend, he said, "Yah, I'm the head of the house but Hilda's the neck that turns the head!" It was true but it didn't matter anymore. The two old people sat there in the twilight among their memories until it was time to go to bed.

Next morning Hilda kissed him and baked up a storm: cookies, cake, cinnamon rolls, new bread, everything that Eino liked. He wandered around for a while, then went down to his boat at Lake Tioga to troll for northern pike. He caught two and they had them for supper. For a fiftieth golden anniversary, it had been a quiet day.

After supper, a very good one, Eino said, "I got present for you, Hilda. I hide it in loft." He got the ladder out and put it in place.

"Yah, Eino, I know," she said. "I got one for you up there too. You bring them both down.

Hilda opened her box first. It contained a six place setting of blue willow ware china. Eino had ordered it from Sears Roebuck after long thought and the perusing of many pages of the catalog.

When she finished unwrapping the last piece of china, Hilda was giggling so hard she almost dropped it. "Open your box, Eino!" she said.

In it was another identical six-place setting of blue willow ware. They had a hard time putting all the pieces out on the table. "We rich, Eino!" she cried. "We very rich! Look!"

Just then there came the damndest yelling and banging of pans from outside the house. *"Chivari! Chivari!"* people yelled, and pounded on the door. All the neighbors were there, celebrating their golden anniversary.

And so was John, their son, carrying four blue willow ware coffee mugs on a blue willow ware platter.

THE NEW CABIN

Only one rich man lived in our little forest village. Perhaps, by modern standards, he wasn't really rich but he had raha (money) in the bank and since he'd retired, he'd been able to take his wife to Florida in February. That man was George Trelawny, but we always called him Captain Jarge because he'd been the mining captain in our town before they shut down the mine in 1912. Captain Jarge was a big, bluff man, rosy cheeked, and born to command. He'd made most of his money buying and selling copper mining stocks on the basis of tips from the diamond drillers who, like him, were also Cousin Jacks, Cornishmen from the old country. Captain Jarge was also a very shrewd judge of men.

That was why the whole town buzzed when they heard that he had picked Billy Manton, of all people, to build a new cabin for his daughter near his own house on Easy Street. We called it Easy Street, not because it meant affluence, but because it was the only street in town without a hill. No, people just couldn't understand it. Everybody knew that old Billy was shiftless and lazy and not at all reliable. He'd had some experience, having helped Untilla build a cabin for some summer people, but Billy had to be supervised all the time, Untilla said.

We kids liked old Billy, not only because he told us interesting stories of the old logging days and river drives, but because he'd drop everything to go fishing with us, or to play mumbletypeg with our jacknives. Billy was sure good at mumbletypeg. He could go up the whole series of acts and his knife point went headfirst into the ground every time. Why, he could even hold the knife point on his scalp or tongue and then flip it with the other hand so it made exactly three somersaults before entering the earth. Billy could do that even on his knees or standing straight up with his eyes closed. That's something!

Anyway Billy liked kids and we liked him. Not many big folks like to play.

Bill Manton's own house was a tar paper shack almost as disreputable as he was. Having been patched often, the big tin washers that held the nails were staggered all over the place and there were boards and sheets of tin at the craziest angles. A disgrace to the town, people said. In the winter though it was snug and warm because Billy covered it with huge heaps of snow. All of our houses in the winter had banks of snow over the foundations to keep them warmer but Billy's shack was more of an igloo than a house. Almost a cave in a huge mound of snow, only the stovepipe, the door and a small south window could be seen. Back of it was a woodshed and an outhouse, both of which were ramshackle. Nevertheless, we kids often dropped in to see Billy in his snow cave on our way back from skiing for it was always warm inside. He never gave us anything to eat, but he'd open up the front of his box stove and tell us stories by the flickering flames.

My father, the doctor, was up at Captain Jarge's house when Billy was asked to build the new cabin because Mrs. Trelawny was having another of her frequent ailments. So Dad couldn't help but overhear the conversation. "Billy," said Captain Jarge, "I want you to build me a good cabin, ten by twenty, one room, double bunk, three window and one door. It's for my daughter, Marian, who's lost her husband and may come up here to stay if I've got a place for her. If she doesn't, well I'll sell it. You know that lot I have, four houses down from here. That's where I want you to put it up. Make it like that cabin you and Untilla built. I've seen it and it's a good one."

Billy hesitated. Looked like a lot of work and would spoil his summer but he changed his mind when Captain Jarge pulled out a big roll of bills from his pocket and laid ten of them on the table. All hundred dollar bills! Billy's eyes popped. He'd never seen that much money in his life. Hell, he'd never seen anything larger than a fiver.

"Well, do you want the job or don't you?" Captain Jarge was getting irritated. "That's plenty of money, more than enough for a helluva good cabin, People will say that I oughtn't to trust you, especially since my wife and I are leaving tomorrow to spend the summer in Cornwall, in the old country, where I came from as a lad of thirteen. Ay, 'twill be good going back and 'aving a spot of they tansy tea, and kippered herring and kidney pie, and seeing tinkle bells on every cottage gate. And saffron buns and they real pasties." Captain Jarge interrupted himself. "Doctor, you sure the trip won't be too hard on the little woman, going by ship and all?"

"Be good for her," my father replied. "Good salt air and a real change of scenery can do wonders. Your wife isn't really sick. I promise you she'll be a new person once she gets out of the house."

All this time Billy had been looking at the money on the table. "Sure, Cap'n," he said at last. "I'll take the job. God knows I need some biting money. Had a hell of a time making it through this last winter. Anything else you want to tell me about it.?"

"No," said Captain Jarge. "Build it as good as you can - as if it were going to be your own house. And get it done before I come back the middle of September so you can hand me the key for the lock and say 'there she is' and say it proud. Well, man, don't diddle. Take the money and get going!" Billy left.

"It's none of my business, Jarge, but aren't you taking quite a gamble on that deal?" My father was still in shock.

"Not as much as you think, Doctor. I know what I'm doing. Besides, I owe old Billy something. Remember the time long ago when my boy Tim fell through the ice on the Beaver Dam and Billy pulled him out. Yes, and wrapped the kid in his own coat and brought him up the hill in that bitter cold? And wouldn't take a penny for it. But as you say, it's none of your business. It's mine. See you again when we get back from the old country."

All that money bothered Billy as he walked back to his shack. At first, he just carried the fat roll of bills in his hand but then he became afraid he'd meet someone so he crammed it into his side pants pocket. But as he walked, that loosened the roll and he looked down to see that a hundred dollar bill was half way out of the pocket. Finally, he put it inside his shirt. "A thousand bucks!" he said to himself. "What the hell will I do with it?"

Our town had no bank and the only honest money-keeper was Higley, the owner of our one saloon. Billy considered that recourse but he knew he'd start drinking if he went down there and besides it was kind of nice being able to feel all that folding money. Tired of thinking about the problem, he finally put the bills in an empty tobacco can and buried it behind the outhouse. Then that worried him too. A rain might wet those bills or someone might dig up the can when he wasn't home. Finally, he fastened the bills with a big safety pin to the inside of his long johns next to his chest. They rustled when he walked and he could pat them to know they were there. Even if one came loose, it would just fall down into his crotch. That took care of that!

Getting going on the cabin was more difficult. Billy went up to the Captain's lot and staked out the foundation area. Ten by twenty, Jarge had said, but was that inside or outside? Should he dig a trench all around and fill it with rocks from the mine and then pour cement to hold them in place so the bottom logs could rest solid and wouldn't rot? It tired Billy just to think of all that hard work. Shouldn't he scoop the surface dirt from the enclosure and replace it with sand so the floor joists wouldn't decay? Cabins sure got a mildew stink when they were built on ground. The answer again was yes, but when Billy started scraping, he hit some big roots and stones. To hell with that! Captain Jarge wouldn't know what was under the floor.

What kind of logs would he use and where would he get them? Cedar, white cedar, would be the best but they would be hell to get out of the swamp and besides they tapered too fast. Spruce? Yeah, that would be OK but there'd be a lot of branch cutting and knots. Perhaps he could get some spruce logs from some jobber who was putting up a carload of pulp wood. Decisions! Decisions! Billy was plumb worn out with all that thinking, and more miserable than he'd been for years. So he unpinned one of the hundred dollar bills from his undershirt, took it down to Higley's Saloon and went on a ten day drunk.

After he survived, and the hangover hemlock knot inside his skull had dissolved, Billy started building the cabin. He soon realized that he would have to hire help so he got Pierre Lafond to take his team and lumber wagon and cut and skid four big twenty-foot cedar logs out of the swamp and haul them to the site. That job also meant buying a new one-man cross-cut saw, a peavey and a chain and there went a lot of another hundred dollar bill! A lot of sweat and hard work! Billy went to Untilla's house and told him he'd pay him four dollars a day to help him on the cabin.

"No!" said the big Finn. "Me have you for a boss? You crazy. I no work for you for ten dollar a day. Got bellyful of you on other cabin. No!" Billy tried to get several other men but was again refused. Finally, he was able to hire several high school kids, including me, for two dollars a day.

Our first job was to lay the cedar foundation logs after peeling off their bark and smoothing off the top edges so they would lie level. That meant Billy had to buy a broad axe and a draw knife because, although he tried, no one would lend him any tools. They knew Billy Manton and besides there had always been an unwritten law in our town that you never asked to borrow a man's tools. Why, you'd might as well ask to borrow his wife.

There were plenty of men in our village who owned spirit levels, those with the bubble in the viewing area that had to be right in the center if the log was truly level but no one would let Billy have the use of one. "Use a bread pan level," they told him. So Billy bought a bread pan, scribed a line around the inside an inch from the top, and filled it with water exactly to the line before he put it on the foundation log. It worked but it took a lot of time and some of the water was always spilling as he moved it from place to place as we hewed the log to even it up. Finally, he said, "To hell with it, boys. We'll just do it by eye from now on." Those bottom logs never were really level, nor, for that matter, were any of the other ones.

Our next job was to cut and haul the other logs that were needed: eighteen twenty-footers and eighteen more that were ten feet long. To the profound disgust of almost everybody in town, Billy cut them from a stand of poplar near the old stagecoach road. Poplar? Poplar for a cabin? Sure it was easy to cut and had few limbs and not much taper, but even well dried, poplar logs decayed fast. Wet green ones would show dry rot in just a year or two. Billy didn't give a damn about what people said. "Easy does it," was his motto. "I'll put up Jarge's cabin but I'm not going to kill myself doing it." He was already tired of the whole job.

Building a cabin out of poplar was bad enough but when the towns people saw that Billy was not going to notch or dovetail his logs, but instead was using the V-box and pole construction, they were outraged. That was only used when you were in a hurry or when the shelter was expected to be temporary - as in building a shack along a trap line. Sure, it was an easy way. You simply nailed two 2 x 6 inch boards together at right angles to form a V, then stood this trough upright in the corner, and as each log was set into place, you put a couple of spikes through the board into the end of the log.

Even with notches and seasoned logs, a cabin takes two or three years to really settle and it's good it does because it just makes the cabin tighter. Not so with Billy's method. Even if the spikes held, which often they would not if a heavy load of snow built up on the roof, it was certain that there would be big gaps between the logs in a short time. What was worse, Billy didn't use ten inch spikes. They were too hard to drive into the logs, he said. Instead, he used four inch nails, sometimes only two to a log. A crazy business! People made bets that the building would fall apart the first winter.

To get lumber for the roof, and the flooring, and to have windows and doors, Billy bought Mrs. Rameaux's old abandoned house. It was in bad shape and needed to be torn down anyway. We kids did most of the demolishing and salvaging. It wasn't worth the two hundred bucks Billy paid for it, because a lot of the boards were warped or cracked or split and all of them had hundreds of nails that we had to pull out or pound in. Pretty junky stuff, but after we painted them, it was hard to know how bad they were.

I'm not going to go into all the shoddy details of how that cabin was built. The floor joints were toe-nailed into the foundation logs, not inserted into notches that had to be chiseled. For chinking between the logs, Billy used ordinary cement mortar instead of wood fiber plaster. "Won't make any difference," he said. "As them poplar logs shrink, it'll fall out anyway and have to be done again, maybe in a year or two." The roof boards did not fit flush with each other and Billy didn't even cover them with tar paper before we put on the shingles. "No need to use two nails per shingle," Billy ordered. "One's enough."

"The hell it is!" roared Mullu's father when he saw what we were doing. "You got to have anyway two per shingle or they'll shift sidewise. And what the hell you doing overlapping them only two inches?" He was so mad, he made Mullu quit the job right then and there. "I no having you learn all wrong," he said. Billy just hired another kid and finally the job was done. We weren't proud. We had some money to buy school clothes and that was about all.

Even Billy wasn't too happy when he looked at the completed cabin and realized that Captain Jarge would be coming home soon. With only three left of the hundred dollar bills still pinned to his underwear, he thought for a long time before he bought a ten gallon pail of yellow paint and swabbed it all over the cabin, inside and out. He used two coats, and they really helped. Indeed, it really didn't look too bad sitting there in the sunshine. Of course, painting those peeled poplar logs would just make them rot all the faster because it would seal the moisture in. Billy didn't care. As he had said when we tried to argue him out of using green maple poles for the floor joists instead of seasoned two by eights, "What Jarge can't see, Jarge won't know."

Summer and potato picking time were over when Captain George Trelawny and his wife returned. Billy had to fortify himself down at Higley's Saloon before going up to confront him and he walked up the hill pretty slowly when he finally had to.

"Got the cabin done, Captain Jarge," he said. "And here's the key so you can go see it."

"No," said Jarge. "The key is yours and so is the house. Now you can move out of that crummy shack and have a decent place to live. And I no longer owe you for saving my son."

STINKER

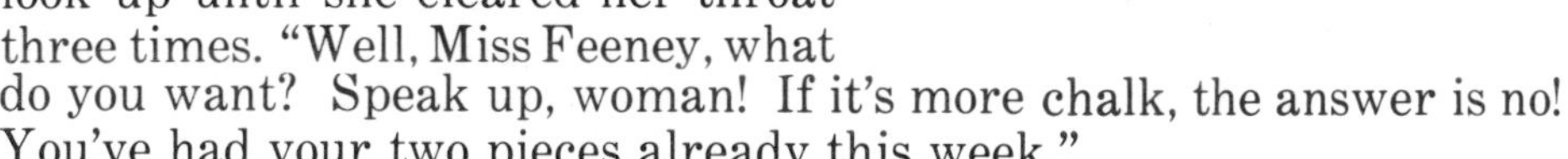

Miss Feeney got to school early that morning and went directly to old Blue Ball's office. B.B. Donegal, our tough school superintendent, was already there, of course, but he didn't look up until she cleared her throat three times. "Well, Miss Feeney, what do you want? Speak up, woman! If it's more chalk, the answer is no! You've had your two pieces already this week."

"No, Mr. Donegal," she answered. "I come for some help and advice, sir. I have a problem and I just don't know how to handle it."

"Come to the point, Miss Feeney. Come to the point! The children will be arriving soon and I want you there when they do!" Old Blue Balls always sounded irritable.

"Well, it's because Theophilus Tissait, the boy the children call Fisheye, comes to school smelling very strong of... of cow manure and it's really causing some difficulties. The girls refuse to sit near him and they hold their noses and ..."

"I know that boy well," he interrupted. "I've had to thrash him more than once. Always into some trouble."

"But, Mr. Donegal, he's a good boy, really. And he's smart. A whiz at mathematics! He can do three place multiplication in his head and I've seen him working out algebra and geometry problems he got from the high school pupils. I don't think he sould be punished for smelling the way he does, although at times it's awfully strong. I just want to know how I should handle the problem."

"I'll take care of it, Miss Feeney. I'll take care of it."

As she left, the teacher regretted having come to him. She liked Fisheye and she was worried about what old Blue Balls might do. A rough man, Mr. Donegal was.

About a half hour after our classes began, the classroom door opened and there he was in the flesh. All of us froze in our seats. "Continue! Continue!" he roared, "and Theophilus, come here, young man!" You could almost hear the sigh of relief from everyone but Fisheye. That unhappy boy got up from his desk and went over to the superintendent, who turned him around several times, sniffing as he did so, then led the boy out of the room. We looked at each other. Poor Fisheye, he'd been up to something and was going to get it good again. A slapping, or maybe the ruler across the hand? Or even the strap? Those of us who had known them ached for poor Fisheye!

But we were wrong. The superintendent merely marched the boy down the hill to his home, gave his mother bloody hell for not sending the boy to school clean, told her to give him a real bath and send him back in a change of clothes. That was all. Didn't hit him once.

When Fisheye didn't return either that morning or that afternoon, I went down to his home. He was my friend. We'd had a lot of good times together and he, with Mullu and me, had rung the schoolbell on that Halloween night when they declared the curfew. A good fishing and trapping partner too. We'd just built a live trap to catch spring rabbits and had planned to put it down in the swamp that very afternoon. And, of course, I wondered what had happened.

When I got there I went up to the back door. (In the U.P., no one ever entered the front door except when there was a funeral.) When his mother opened it, she told me Fisheye was in the cowbarn. "Wait a minute, Cully," she said. "Fisheye didn't eat anything this noon and he must be hungry. Take this piece of bread out to him." She smeared the slice with lard, then sprinkled some salt and a dusting of sugar over it.

I found my friend huddled on some hay, wrapped in a dirty old blanket, and naked. Although it was a fine spring day, it was still in the lower fifties, a mite cold to be that way without clothes. So I asked him how come. He explained what had happened and said that since he had no change of clothes and his mother had now washed his old ones and had them hanging on the line, he'd have to wait until they were dry. He also said that his mother told him he'd have to go back to sleeping on the hard kitchen floor at night like he did in winter time rather than in the soft hay, at least until school was finished for the year.

The Tissaits were dirt poor and they had a lot of kids, three girls and four boys, Fisheye being the oldest. The girls slept together in one corner of the loft and the younger three boys in the other, so Fisheye was odd man out. None of them ever had enough to eat either and maybe that was why Fisheye was the smallest boy in our class. But he was very strong and tough and not afraid of anything. A good fighter, too.

I, myself, had never noticed that he smelled bad though probably others did. Most of us by spring were pretty high in body odor anyway. I guess the tar oil or bear grease used on our boots to waterproof them during the break-up masked all other smells. I could understand though that Fisheye, if he slept in that cowbarn, would acquire an extra aroma because the cow's stall was still full of the winter's crap. I shoveled some of it out onto the pile behind the barn and wished there was something else I could do to help.

On my way home, I suddenly realized that unless Fisheye had another set of clothes, he'd soon be in trouble again. So when I got there, I went to my room and bundled up an old, but clean, shirt of mine and some pants, underwear and socks for him because I had extras. My mother, however, caught me sneaking down the backstairs with them and wanted to know what I was up to. When I told her the whole story and how unfair it was, she agreed but she vetoed giving Fisheye my old clothes. "Let's get him some new ones," she said. "He's about your size, isn't he, Cully? But then she asked me if Fisheye or his mother would be sensitive about accepting them. You had to be very careful in the U.P. not to hurt a person's pride. We were a proud people. I told her about the bread smeared with lard and how Fisheye insisted on my having a piece of it before he'd eat any. Anyway, mother decided to go to Flinn's store immediately, buy a whole new outfit for Fisheye, get Father Hassel, their priest, to deliver it, and not to tell the Tissaits who had sent it.

Miss Feeney was delighted when Fisheye arrived in school the next morning in a new red plaid shirt, wool pants, new shoes and socks and even a real belt instead of the piece of clothesline that had previously held up his tattered overalls. He'd also been scrubbed until he shone and his hair had been cut. Altogether he looked pretty good and certainly the old cow smell was gone. No one said anything, of course.

I noticed though that at recess Fisheye didn't go down with us to the ditch of the little creek that flowed through the schoolyard into a culvert under our hill street. Playing lumberjacks, we were building logging dams and floating little sticks in the pond behind them. Fisheye watched us but said he didn't want to get dirty.

However, when school let out that afternoon, he got dirty anyway. It happened like this. Walter Donegal, old Blue Ball's youngest boy, started calling Fisheye names and picking a fight with him. "Hi, cowshit," he said. "Hi, stinker! So my old man had to take you out of school to get a bath, hey? Stinky, stinky, double stinky!" Walter had been a nice kid when he was younger and I used to play with him a lot even though he was one grade up from me. But he'd developed a cruel streak and was always bullying kids who were smaller than he was. Maybe it was because his father was also cruel and beat him up more than he should have done.

Anyway, after Fisheye took it for a while, he came out swinging. He was a pretty good fighter for his size, too, but this time he didn't have a chance, Walter being at least a head taller. He gave Fisheye a hard poke in the nose that set it bleeding. Fisheye didn't give up and tried to close in but Walter knocked him down. "Fight! Fight!"yelled the kids and soon there was a ring of us about the two of them, screaming and urging Fisheye on. It was no contest although Fisheye got in a couple of good licks to the body before he stayed down on the ground crying helplessly. Walter gave him one last hard kick and then everyone left but Fisheye and me. I'd sure wanted to join the scrap but the first rule of fighting in the U.P. was that it had to be one on one. No fair having anyone help you. The second rule was: No fair kicking in the crotch!

I sure felt sorry for Fisheye. His nose was still bleeding and one eye was swelling but the worst of it was that his fine new store clothes were a mess and he was afraid to go home. So I brought him up to our house and explained to Mother what had happened.

As always, she came through just the way she should have. She soaked one of Dad's gauze pads in cold water and had Fisheye hold it on his swellings. She washed off his face tenderly and kept talking to him nice and sweet as she took off the dirty shirt, sponged away the dirt and then ironed it. Then she gave each of us a big fat sugar cookie and a glass of milk as she brushed all the dirt from his pants. Pretty soon, Fisheye was cleaned up and except for his eye, no one would have known he'd been in a fight. Mother also gave him a little bag of chocolate candies, one for each of his brothers and sisters and two for his mother, and five for you, Fisheye, she said. So everything worked out all right.

Indeed, it did, for that next Sunday evening, Old Blue Balls smelled skunk coming up from his basement and found a big old striper in it with tail raised on high. Furious, he gave Walter a hard thrashing for not closing the cellar door as he'd been told to do, then ordered him to get the varmint out of there. We heard all about it from Mrs. Donegal when she came to ask my mother how to get the skunk smell out of clothing.

"You know my husband, Mrs. Gage," Walter's mother said. "He's got a terrible temper and when Walter refused to grab the skunk by the tail and carry it outside, I really feared for the boy, I did, Mrs. Gage, his father was beating him so hard. But Walter wouldn't do it and he claimed he'd shut that cellar door right after his father had told him to do it. Well, Mr. Donegal (she always referred to her husband in that formal way) tried to shoo the critter out but it wouldn't shoo and that made him so mad he got his shotgun and blasted the skunk to smithereens. But oh, Mrs. Gage, my house smells terrible and Walter does too because his father made him scoop up the remains and bury them in the garden. It's been a bad day, Mrs. Gage."

When Mother told her she'd heard that it was wise to bury all the clothing in a hole and cover it with dirt and leave it there three days before trying to wash it, Mrs. Donegal said that she wished she could do the same with both Walter and Mr. Donegal. "I tried to tell them that if they'd just leave the cellar door open overnight, the skunk would go away, but no, Mr. Donegal just had to shoot it. It's awful to have to live with a man who has a temper like Mr. Donegal," she complained. She also asked to borrow one of Mother's copper boilers. "We'll have to have a lot of hot water for all the bathing as has to be done right away," she said as she departed.

The next morning it was evident that all the scrubbing hadn't helped Walter too much. He sure stank and the kids he couldn't lick began to call him "Stinky," a label he carried with him, without pleasure, all of his school days. And for a long time afterwards, whenever it rained, the Donegal's house stunk again of skunk and Walter got another thrashing from his father for not closing that cellar door.

Or perhaps he had closed it! All I know is that when Fisheye and I went down into the swamp below Company Field hill to put out the livetrap for spring rabbits, using an old carrot for bait, I noticed that the trap smelled pretty strong of skunk. Maybe that's why we never caught a rabbit in it.

THE RICH MAN

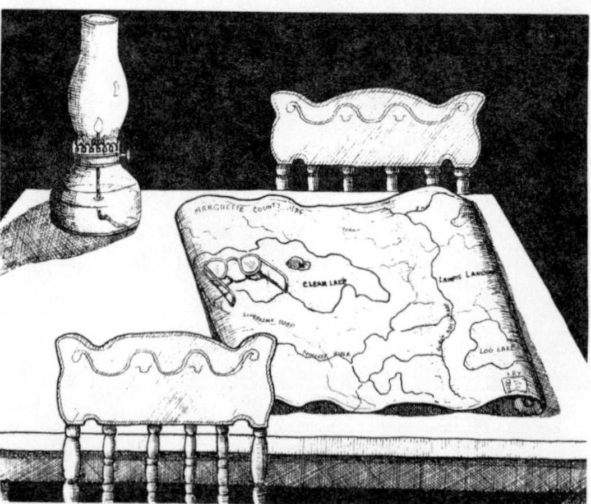

It was in the early summer that the rich man from Chicago came to town and asked my father, the village doctor and township supervisor, about buying Clear Lake. "I've made a pile of money," he said, "and I want to play with it. I want a lake with an island in it on which I can build a fine fishing and hunting lodge for myself and to entertain my business associates. I talked last month with Carter Harrison, the Mayor of Chicago, who, as you know, has such a retreat up on the Log Lake, and he was very enthusiastic about the fishing and hunting up here."

He'd already made a mistake, the first of many to come. Strangers were always supposed to give their names and identify themselves upon first encounter. We in the U.P. were always a bit suspicious about strangers, especially those from down below. Dad asked him his name.

"I'm James Daney, Chicago Board of Trade," the man answered impatiently and a bit arrogantly. "I've looked over these maps, (he spread two of them out on our dining table) and the lakes I've marked with a cross look like possibilities. What I want to know, my good man, is whether any of them have a two or three acre island in it."

My father stiffened. "I'm not your good man," he said curtly, "and you'll mind your manners, sir or I'll show you the door!"

Mr. Daney apologized perfunctorily. "I'm used to doing business in a hurry, I guess, Doctor." he said, "but I'd appreciate it if you'd look at these maps. All I want to know is which of these lakes has an island in it.

Dad relented and looked at the maps. "The only one that might fit your requirements is this one, Clear Lake. It's about six miles north of here and about one mile from the nearest road."

"But look, Doctor, the map shows a road running right by the lake."

Mr. Daney pointed to a faint dotted line.

"Oh, that's just an old logging road used in the days when they cut the big pine. It's all overgrown now, completely impassible. The closest you could get to the lake by horse and buggy is here at Lampi's Clearing. You'd have to hike in the rest of the way and it's rough going."

"But the island, Doctor, the island? Are you sure there's a good sized island in it?"

"Of course, I'm sure," Dad said irritably. "I've fished that lake and hunted around it for twenty years. The island's about maybe four acres in size and has some virgin cork pines on it."

"Good! I'll go see it. I presume your town has a livery stable?" Dad nodded. "Then, sir, can you find me a guide? I never buy a pig in a poke. Got to see it with my own eyes."

Dad was fed up with him. "No," he said, "I have to call on some patients. Find your own guide." He didn't want any rich man from Chicago buying Clear Lake. After all, he and B.B. Donegal had lugged a milk can full of tiny Northern Pike through that nasty country to plant the lake and it now had some real lunkers in it.

Marchand told my father later that he'd given the man old Maude and the oldest buggy he had in the barn. Marchand even had to tell him the difference between "Gee!" and "Haw!" and show him how to hold the reins. "Cette homme, he know nossing about horses," Marchand said. The stranger had tried to hire him to drive Maude up to Clear Lake and guide him in to it but the old Frenchman had refused. Nor did he know of anyone who could or would. This was haying time and the men who weren't making hay were cutting wood or fishing. Marchand told him he might find some loafer at Higley's Saloon who'd still be sober enough to take him up there.

So that was where Mr. Daney went first. The saloon was on the far side of the railroad tracks at the bottom of the hill, but, because he pulled the right rein when he had to make the left turn, he ended up at Paddy Feeny's blacksmith shop instead. There he blustered in, and explained what he wanted in some detail while Paddy was doing some rather delicate work on a broken chain hoist. Now, our blacksmith was something of an artist and we all knew that he wasn't to be interrupted when white hot iron from the forge was ready to be worked. We knew that,but the man from Chicago didn't. Impatiently, he began to repeat what he had said until Paddy grabbed his tongs and chased him out of the shop, roaring like only a mad Irishman can.

At the saloon, Higley wasn't much help either. "What the hell you want to buy that godforsaken pond in the hills for?" he asked. "There's no road into it and it'd cost a fortune to make one over those damned granite hills and through the swamps. Why don't you buy a piece on Lake Tioga?" No, he didn't know of anyone who'd guide him. The only one who might was Alphonse Moreau but he was down sick and if he had been well, he'd have laughed his head off at the idea of taking that city dude with the straw hat up in the bush. Besides, the fool hadn't even bought a beer. To hell with him!

Mr. Daney was getting frustrated but he was so determined he began to stop at some of the houses to inquire. Unfortunately, he knocked at the front doors instead of going around to the back, as we always did in the U.P. Although several lace curtains fluttered, only old lady Bisset came to see who was there, and when she saw the straw hat and necktie and fancy clothes and pointed shoes, she let out a bunch of hostile French jargon, then slammed the door in his face.

Beginning to feel a bit hungry, Mr. Daney drove up the hill street looking for a restaurant or cafe and, of course, found nothing. When the mine was running many years before, he might have had a good meal at the Beacon House, but it was boarded up and decaying. As old Maude plodded up the hill, Mr. Daney met a bunch of kids going home to their dinner meal and he stopped the horse to ask where the restaurant was. The children milled around the buggy but they just shook their head. "Then is there a store up here?" he asked. As one kid nodded and pointed up the street, some angry woman came out of a nearby house and gave them hell in a torrent of half English, half Finnish, the children scattered. We watched over our children in the U.P.

When Mr. Daney entered Flinn's General Store, Mr. Flinn took one look at his get up and told him in no uncertain terms that he didn't need any salesman trying to sell him a bill of goods, that he had his own suppliers. And when the man from Chicago asked about a cafe, he sold him a link of bologna, some cheese and crackers and a bottle of red pop. One dollar and seventy cents. No, Mr. Flinn didn't know anyone who might guide him to Clear Lake.

We'd had our noon meal when the stranger appeared again at our door. "Doctor," he said. "I've been unable to find a guide but I'm bound to see that lake. I have just one question: how will I know when I've got to Lampi's Clearing where the trail to Clear Lake starts?"

Dad tried to dissuade him. "You can't go in there by yourself. It's wild country. You'll get lost."

"Nonsense!" Mr. Daney replied. "I've got this map and it's only a mile. I tell you, Doctor, I'm going to see that lake."

"It's only a mile as a crow flies," Dad said. "But it's a lot longer by trail. The trail isn't easy to follow either and I have no urge to assemble a search crew to find some fool from Chicago up in that country. I'd bet you don't even have a compass and it's beginning to cloud up. You wouldn't have a chance, man. No!"

Mr. Daney was not to be deterred. "All right, sir. I'll have to take that chance. According to my map, that clearing must be about five miles up the road. I'll look for it and the trail. Good day, sir!"

Dad relented. "No, you mustn't do it!" he said. "You just don't understand what you're tackling." Then he turned to me.

"Cully," he said, "how about you taking him in to Clear Lake?" I nodded. "My son has been up there often, not only with me but with his friends. He knows the way as well as any man." I sure felt good to hear that praise.

Mr. Daney was relieved. "Fine, fine!" he said. "I'll pay him five dollars for guiding me."

"No," Dad replied. "That's a man's wages. Two dollars would be plenty."

So off we went in the old buggy with Maude plodding down the hill street, her head bobbing up and down with every step. But then I suddenly thought of something. "Mister," I said. "We'd better go back to Marchand's livery stable and get a halter and a rope. We'll have to leave Maude in the Clearing for two or three hours and she can't graze good with the bridle on. We'll tie her to the back of the wagon. That's the way we always do it. Keeps them from straying, too."

The man from Chicago vetoed the suggestion. "Ah, hell," he said, "That decrepit old nag won't stray. We'll be lucky if she just gets us there and back." He yelled at Maude and slapped her back with the reins but the old horse didn't move any faster.

It seemed like a long trip even if it were only six miles and Mr. Daney didn't talk much except to cuss the horse for her slowness. When we got to the pool below the spring, Maude made for it, of course, and had a long drink despite his yelling. Once he got off the rig and walked alongside for a spell, then had to run to catch up, and was mad all over again.

Finally, we got to Lampi's Clearing and Mr. Daney marked it on the map. He couldn't wait to jump out of the buggy, and we left it right out in the open and where there wasn't any shade. Not much for the horse to eat where we stopped either.

"C'mon! C'mon, boy. Let's go! Show me the trail!" The man from Chicago sure had burrs under his saddle. I led him to where the trail started behind the big rock but then he insisted on going first. Not for long, though, because he kept losing it and wandering off into the brush. Why he even argued with me when I refused to go down a well worn deer trail that crossed our route. A heavy man, Mr. Daney was soon sweating and so the deer flies began to bite him good. I offered him my extra red bandanna to put under his hat but he refused even though the back of his neck was getting bloody. He stumbled a lot too. Sure didn't know how to walk in the woods. Never looked at the ground or felt it with his feet like we did and he tried to plunge ahead too fast. I don't know how many times an alder branch knocked off that silly straw hat of his or how often a dry spruce limb raked his face. I do know that he fell heavily to the ground three times before we even hit the stream that flowed out of the lake.

Clear Creek, where the trail crossed it, is fairly good sized, maybe thirteen feet wide. The crossing comes at a place where the beavers once had a big dam, one that had washed out long ago, but there still was a deep muddy pool behind the part of it that remained. I knew of only two ways to handle it. One was to take a running jump to the big rock part way to the other side and then another jump to shallow water near the old dam. The other way was to go down below and wade across, fighting an immense tangle of windfalls and underbrush. I had no trouble getting across by jumping, but Mr. Daney didn't want to tackle it rny way. It must have been ten or fifteen minutes later that he rejoined me and was glad to sit down. How he looked really worried me. Mr. Daney's face was beet red and the jowls on his jowls were purple. He was also breathing hard as he showed me how he had torn his coat and pants in that awful tangle.

But after a little rest, he was ready to go again, though he groaned when he got to his feet. "According to the map," he said, "we ought to be crossing that logging road soon. Even though it runs to the far end of the lake, I think we'll take it. Certainly, can't be any worse than this damned trail."

I tried to argue him out of it when we came to the old logging road although at that place it was fairly well defined. "The trail is a lot shorter," I said, "and pretty soon the old road turns into a swamp full of alders and almost disappears." But Mr. Daney would have none of it. Sure was a bull headed bugger.

Well, he got a good introduction to alder bushes when we hit that swamp. They knocked off his straw hat a million times; they tangled up his arms; they tripped him. When he tried by sheer force to bull his way through they knocked him down, and, of course, soon he had lost the old ruts completely. I followed and waited until he finally came to his senses, then led him out of the swamp up onto high ground and back to the trail again. There Mr. Daney had to sit down for a time. "How much further, boy? How much further?" he panted and he asked to borrow the bandanna he'd refused before. The mosquitoes had been pretty fierce down there in the swamp.

Nothing much happened from there to the lake except that he lost a shoe once in the muskeg and took a hard tumble coming down that last steep granite hill. Finally, I led him out onto Hedet Point, a big rocky ledge that jutted out into the lake with deep water on both sides.

For several minutes, Mr. Daney just stood there with his mouth open, taking it all in. "Lord, what a beautiful spot!" he said. "It's worth all that hell of getting in. And look at that island. Just perfect!" He sat down heavily on the stone on which hundreds of our men and kids had sat after heaving out a big bobber with a minnow on it. "Son," he said. "this is it! Just what I wanted. But is there a spring somewhere around so I can have a drink? I'm sure thirsty."

"No," I told him. "But the lake is spring fed, with spring water coming in under the surface. The water is good to drink. Here!" I dipped in my felt hat and drank some to show him it was all right.

Mr. Daney was dubious about drinking out of my hat so I got some birch bark, made a cone of it, folded it in half and clinched it with a small branch slit lengthwise. He was surprised to see that it held water and he drank three dippers full before he had enough. Again he feasted his eyes on the lake.

Clear Lake is a pretty lake though there are hundreds as good or better in the U.P. It lies in a bowl of granite hills and on a quiet day like this one every feature of the skyline was reflected in the water, the spires of spruce, the taller pines, the white birch and the soft fluffy tops of cedars, everything. Fifty shades of green could be seen in that blue lake and it seemed full to the brim under the labrador tea bushes that surrounded it. Then there was the island with its great pines only 150 yards off the point where we were sitting and white pond lilies on their flat green pads down below us. Yes, it was beautiful, all right.

Mr. Daney began talking to himself. "Yeah," he said. "That island is just right. We'll build a raft ferry to it with a long rope going over wheels at each end. And we'll have a big boathouse right here with the canoes and boats and fishing tackle. And behind us will be the men's and servants' quarters. And on the island, besides the master cabin, I'll have three or four guest cabins, a big dining kitchen cabin, and another big recreation cabin to hold the library and billiard table and grand piano. Lots of big windows looking over the lake..."

He fell silent and all I could think of was how he'd spoil it.

We sat there a long time as he talked to himself, making plans. "Yes, and we'll build a good road right to this point, and a bridge over that damned stream with a gate across it, and fence in the whole property..."

That was too much for me, so I interrupted his reverie. "Mister," I said, "I sure wouldn't put up any fence or gate if I were you."

"Why not? It'll be my property. Of course, I'll have the place fenced."

I tried to explain that in the U.P. we didn't like fences on land that we'd hunted and fished for years. "Just build your buildings," I said, "and no one will bother you. But if you put up any gate or fence or no trespassing signs, they'll not only tear them down but burn your cabins and dynamite your bridge."

He looked at me as if I were stupid or crazy, so I didn't say anymore. Finally he looked at his watch. "My lord," he said. "It's half past four. We'd better be getting back if I'm to catch that train." Finally, he was willing to let me lead the way.

When we got to Clear Creek again, Mr. Daney decided not to tackle that awful tangle below the beaver dam, but to try jumping it like I did. Unfortunately, his leather shoes by that time were smooth as ice from the leaves and pine needles on which we'd been walking and so, with a wild waving of arms, he fell ass over appetite, plunk into the deep water. When he got to the other side Mr. Daney sure was a mess, muddy, wet to the bone, and sure stinking from the old beaver gunk. His straw hat had fallen off but I hooked it with a stick just before it went down the draw. Oh, how he cussed. I suggested that he take off his clothes and wring them out before we started walking but he just brushed himself off and refused. "Gad, if I ever take my shoes off, I'll never get them on again, my feet are so swollen," he said. He had to sit down several times before we came to the clearing, he was so tired. The last time he sat down, he talked about how good that bologna and rat cheese would taste when we got to the horse and buggy.

But when we finally got out of the bush into the Clearing, there was no horse and buggy. The tracks showed that old Maude had decided to go home. I thought Mr. Daney would weep when he realized what had happened, but all he did was beat his head and swear. He lay on the ground for about ten minutes completely exhausted before he was able to start walking again.

We were fortunate enough to find Maude and the buggy three miles, and an hour and a half, down the road munching grass in a meadow. Although Mr. Daney was too tired to eat, I wasn't and as I drove the rest of the way, I munched the bologna, cheese and crackers as he nodded in the seat beside me. A long way back to town.

We heard the Chicago, Milwaukee and St. Paul train tooting for the cemtery crossing when we were still way up the pike. Mr. Daney looked at his watch, but it was so wet, it had stopped. He slumped in his seat. "I'll miss that train now for sure," he said. "And then what will I do? No hotel or anything else in that godforsaken town. Probably have to spend the night in the depot. Dammit, I could buy that whole town and I won't be able even to find a place to sleep!" I almost felt sorry for the man.

I got off at my house and he paid me five dollars, but didn't say thank you. Later we found out that he slept overnight in Marchand's hayloft under an old horse blanket before catching the South Shore to Negaunee and then the Northwestern Railroad back to Chicago.

For some reason or another, he never came back.

THE OLD, OLD DAYS

In these tales of the old U.P., I have enjoyed remembering the people I knew as a youth in the early years of this century. But even when I was a child, I kept hearing stories of the real old days, of the strong men and gallant women who first migrated to our rough land, fought the elements and each other, and survived. Although the rock of the U.P. is the oldest in the world, the history of its inhabitants is very short. Indeed, most of it has occurred within two lifetimes - that of Sieur La Tour and my own.

La Tour was the oldest man in our forest village of Tioga, a wizened little man but still with black hair and good hearing. He was an uncle of a cousin of Fisheye's and that's how I got to be able to sit there by his cabin to hear him talk about old times. We'd bring him an apple, a half loaf of bread, or some cookies, and then ask him a question. That was all we had to do. He'd just start talking and we'd be there spellbound for hours.

Nobody knew exactly how old LaTour was. He probably didn't either but he was certainly in his late eighties or early nineties because he told us once that he was in his thirties when the Civil War was declared. The old man said according to what his mother had told him that he had been born in a birchbark canoe. His parents had been picking blueberries all day along the shore of Whitefish Bay just west of the Soo where they lived and were coming back when it happened. They weren't even able to make it to shore. That's all he knew about his birth but he did say that he remembered the cradle in which his mother rocked him and the brothers and sisters who came after him. It was made of a whiskey keg, sawed lengthwise so it would rock easily. They had painted it blue.

LaTour's father and grandfather had been trappers and voyageurs, couriers de bois. He recalled his father telling of almost drowning in Lake Superior off Tres Rivieres (Three Rivers) at the western edge of Lake Superior when the long bateau loaded with furs had capsized. One of his grandmothers had been an Ojibway Indian but she had died before he was born.

Sieur LaTour had only a few things to tell about his early years. One spring afternoon we found him sitting on the bench beside his cabin door shaving thin strips from a chunk of white cedar. They were spills, he said. He used them instead of matches to light his pipe if a candle or a fire in the stove were burning. He couldn't forget how valuable matches had been when he was a boy in the Soo. Why, they were even used instead of money for small things.

Just about then a white throated sparrow began to sing in the lilac tree. "Ah, mes amis," the old man said. "Zat bird, she say 'Hard Times In Canady, Canady, Canady.' " It really does sound like that. Then he went on to describe how it was to be poor in the old, old days in Sault St. Marie. His father was usually gone all summer hauling furs in the long canoes, and in the fall or spring he ran a trapline way back in the bush. So Sieur, as the eldest boy, had to play pere and feed the family. Fish was the main staple. There was an eddy in the river by Sugar Island where he fished almost everyday, mainly for trout. Sometimes he'd help the commercial fishermen dry their nets and be given a big lake trout or whitefish for his effort. And always, there were the many *lapin* (rabbits) he caught in snares or livetraps. No beef or pork ever, but venison, *mais certainment,* when his father was home to shoot a deer.

Suddenly the old man remembered a wild trip down the Sault rapids below the outlet of Lake Superior. In a birchbark canoe with an Indian and his father paddling, they had shot those terrible rapids. Sieur's job was to reach over the side of the canoe and scoop up, with a hand net, the whitefish that were swimming upstream. There were thousands of them there in the fast water and he recalled that he was half covered with flopping fish when they got to shore. That, too, was the year of the bad winter when the family almost starved and froze to death. "We fire all day and night and ze water she freeze in ze bucket by the stove."

LaTour remembered the Soo Canal being built because he had a job leading the oxen that dragged timbers to the site. He also recalled how, even before that, he had witnessed a sailing vessel being hauled over the plank and rail *portage* from Lake Huron to Lake Superior. He was "twenty or so" when the locks opened and the copper ore from the Keweenaw and the pig iron from Marquette no longer had to be brought over the portage by cart. With a wheelbarrow, he'd help unload the schooners that brought it to the Soo.

When the next son was old enough to take over his responsibilities, Sieur left home to make his own way in the world. He'd heard many rumors of the rich discoveries of iron, copper, yes, and even gold that were being made in the western part of the U.P. and that there were jobs for anyone who could work. He would go there and make his fortune.

Once, I asked the old man how he'd happened to come to Tioga and he answered that it was probably because of seasickness. He'd saved some money working on the Soo canal and had bought passage in a sailing vessel going to the Copper Country with a cargo of mules, hay bales, and bags of oats. At that time the early copper mines had to bring everything in, food and supplies of every kind. It was in late summer, LaTour siad. After they sailed out of Whitefish Bay, they had encountered one storm after another. He was certain he was about to die, he was so sick.

They put in at the good harbor at Grand Marais and lay anchor for two days and then anchored again at Grand Island (Munising) for three more, waiting for calmer weather. When, instead of continuing to the Copper Country, the ship stopped at Marquette, again because of heavy seas, LaTour staggered ashore, hunted up a priest at the mission there and confessed his sins. He never got on a ship again.

For several years LaTour worked in Marquette or its vicinity but I'm not sure just what he did. He told of wheelbarrowing loads of *couchons* into the holds of sailing vessels at the oredocks. Very heavy work he said. These couchons (pig iron chunks about two feet long, also called 'blooms') had been smelted in the charcoal furnaces south of town.

Once, when we asked the old man how he became a lumberjack, LaTour answered that he started by cutting and hauling hardwood to the beehive kilns near the furnace, the kilns where the charcoal was made. He'd bought his first rifle then. Oh, yes, at another time the old man told us about helping build a plank railroad from the iron mines at Teal Lake to Marquette. Either my memory is faulty or the old man's was too, but this period in his life remains pretty vague.

Always wanting to go to the Copper Country, but unwilling ever to board ship again, LaTour had heard that there was a stagecoach route running from Green Bay to Houghton, so he started to work his way west to intercept it at a tiny settlement near Lake Tioga where they changed horses and had barns and sleeping cabins. It took him many years to do it, most of them spent working at the new iron mines at Negaunee and Ishpeming. He never went underground, though. "Me, I look in zat hole and say, 'Non, Non!' Ze grave, she is for LaTour not yet." There was plenty of hard labor to be done on the surface however and men were scarce.

When he got a chance to join a crew digging exploratory test pits for iron still further west, near Escanaba River, LaTour went along. He remembered vividly the great pine forest on the plains through which the Indian trail passed. Dark there even at noon, he said. No underbrush. No birds singing. When they came to the river and the granite hills, it was good to see the sun again.

But LaTour didn't like that test pit job. Too much down in the hole, he said. He had a mean boss and the food not only was poor, but there was little of it. After about a month, when he had to pack samples of rock back to Ishpeming for assay, he stayed there.

This time, however, he didn't work at the mines. He found he could make more money killing game for the boarding houses at the mining locations. Deer were plentiful and near enough so the dragging was not too bad. He'd get two or three dollars a deer and more if he butchered them. He also trapped a little. It was a good life, the old man said, except in the deep of winter when game got scarce. Then he cut wood.

Hearing that there would be good pay, LaTour also spent a year or two working for the railroads that were pushing into the wilderness. His first job was clearing the right-of-way and then laying track for the Peninsular Railroad which came up from the south to Ishpeming. He also worked on the Marquette, Houghton and Ontonagon Railroads that they were building west from Marquette. LaTour was there tamping railroad ties when the Civil War was declared. He was about thirty years old then.

We asked him if he'd thought of becoming a soldier in that war. No, he said. That war was far away and he was a Canadian. The main effect of the war on the old U.P. was just to increase the feverish demand for iron and copper. Jobs everywhere, the old man said. New mines were being built in every hill.

When the railroad got to the Escanaba River, they had trouble building the bridge and so for a month, he worked building kilns at Clarksburg. He didn't like that kind of work either and, when he almost got killed in the quarry, he quit to join a surveying crew heading westward along the edge of the granite hills. He was a chainman on that job and though it was easy enough compared to the hard labor he'd done before, he got bored doing the same thing over and over, and so again he quit, this time at the settlement that became Tioga, our town.

Already a lot of preliminary work was being done to build a new mine there: clearing the land, erecting cabins and a shaft house on top of our big hill. Down in the valley only a few stables, horse barns, and shacks marked the old stage coach stop but the stage was no longer being operated by the Welsh Brothers of Green Bay. Originally, the stage line had been started to bring mail and the payroll to the soldiers at Fort Wilkins at the end of the Keweenaw Peninsula. In the winter months, these were carried by dogsled. By the time LaTour got to Tioga, the stage coaches had been abandoned and only the winter sledges were still traveling up the old Military Road, as it was called, that skirted the south shore of our lake. Still intent on getting to the Copper Country of his dreams, LaTour once started to walk it but when he got to the big river that flowed out of Lake Tioga, it was a roaring flood. He tried to cross it, he said, but was carried downstream and so went back to Tioga. There he helped build a boarding house near the mine, and then later some of the company houses put up to house a constantly increasing number of miners, many from foreign lands: Cousin Jacks from Cornwall, Finns, Irish, French, and "Hunyaks" from Poland and other mid-eastern countries. Within a few years after the railroad came to Tioga in 1870, more than a thousand men were employed in the mines around the village. LaTour was one of them for a time, but he quit to become a market hunter again.

The demand for meat was so great that the mining company put LaTour and a couple of other men on its payroll to provide it. They also let them keep what other money they got from the boarding houses. He'd never made such good money before or since, the old man said, so he built a cabin down in the valley, and hid his pay of silver dollars in cans buried in the woods behind it. It was all spent now, he said, though perhaps he'd forgotten where he'd put some of the cans. Under his direction Fisheye and I dug around but didn't find any.

One afternoon, LaTour told us hunting stories for hours but I recall only a few of them. He said that when the railroad came with its telegraph wires, he and the other two market hunters cut sections of that wire and used them to snare deer. You had to find a good runway where there was a limber but stout young maple sapling. Then you'd make the loop, place it over the trail and anchor the tip of the sapling on the other side after climbing it to make it fall over. When a deer went into the loop, it would plunge ahead, release the sapling and be thrown. LaTour had caught many deer that way, he said.

He also described the pits he dug in the fall before the big migration. Back then our deer migrated south every fall once the first deep snow came and then in the spring, they'd return northwest to the hills. At that time these runways were old and over a foot deep, LaTour said. In the pits he drove heavy stakes with sharp points and then covered everything with thin balsam branches and leaves. When the snow came, the migrating deer fell into the pits and skewered themselves. Once he got a deer in each of fourteen pits in a single week, covered them up again, and after the next snow, got ten more. Meat for the winter, LaTour said, and no shells to buy that way.

His tale of passenger pigeons interested me most because at home we had a stuffed one in a glass case and they became completely extinct shortly after I was born. A big bird, the size of a barn pigeon, it had a reddish breast almost like that of a robin. There were tremendous flocks of them in the old days, LaTour said, sometimes thousands of birds in a flock. There were so many they'd often break the limbs of the trees they roosted in. "Wen zey come in zey sound lak tonnerre (thunder) and ze sky look lak night come." LaTour would hide in a blind under their favorite roosting trees and shoot them with a ten gauge shotgun, getting many with a single shot. Then the pigeons would circle around and come back and he'd shoot again. On one single day he got enough to fill a barrel with them, all skinned and cleaned. They brought very good moneys, he said.

LaTour spent ten, twelve years doing this market hunting before the game got scarce and it was time to try something new. Having no urge to go back to the hard labor of the mines, he became a lumberjack, riverman and teamster. This was in the 1880's and he kept at it until Read and Company drove the Pesheekee for the last time in 1906 and all the virgin pine forest was gone.

The old man had many tales of his work in the woods, but I just can't remember them. He never was a sawyer for he said that he could make no sense of having to pull and push a saw all day for months at a time. Instead, because he had a way with oxen, he began by skidding the great logs down to the iced river roads with them, and then later he was promoted to be a teamster, hauling supplies from town to the camps. Then when spring came, he started driving logs down the rivers. That was dangerous work, but exciting, he said. He remembered one terrible logjam below Busch's Rapids that built up for days, and he told us of the horror that came when Brown's Dam let go. We heard about those several times but the one story he retold most often was the time they drove logs down the outlet of Lake Tioga right to Menominee and he had to walk back more than a hundred miles before he got home.

When our townspeople asked him to what he attributed his old age, he answered that it was because he had never drunk whiskey and had never got married. He'd had a good life, he said, without either of them.

LaTour finally did get to see the Copper Country, his lifelong dream. He was in his late eighties when he took the train to Houghton, looked around for an hour, then took the next train back to Tioga. Just some more mines, he said.

Those were the old, old days.

P. P. POLSON

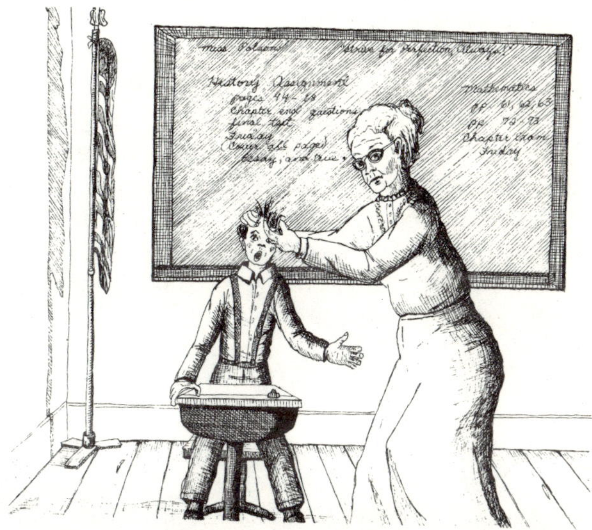

Long before we entered sixth grade, we'd heard about the teacher we were going to get. "Just you wait till you get P. P. for a teacher," the older kids told us. "She's the meanest, toughest teacher in the whole school!" That was saying something too because back then in the old days, teachers were supposed to be hard nosed and they were. With a few exceptions, our teachers were the absolute monarchs of their classrooms, ruling the unruly by the threat or practice of corporal punishment. Parents never complained to the school board if a kid got a whipping in school; they just gave him another trimming after he got home. Uneducated, often illiterate themselves, they prized education as the one hope they had that their children might have better lives than their own. Teachers were looked up to in our town. Men took off their hats, and women curtsied when they met them on the sidewalks.

I'll never forget that first day of sixth grade. We filed in, took seats as far back in the classroom as we could, and covertly looked our teacher over. A big, strong Swede woman, P. P. Polson did not look up from the papers on her desk until the bell clanged. Then she went to the middle of the reciting platform in front of the blackboard, gave us a terrible glare, and said, "I'm Miss Polson, your teacher. You are my pupils, and don't forget it. I am determined that you will get an education whether you like it or not. I have rules and the first rule is that when I speak you will all sit up straight and pay attention." Whereupon she marched briskly down to where Arvo sat slumped in his seat, grabbed him up by the hair and dangled him at arm's length. He was a big kid, too. When Arvo let out a howl, she slapped him hard across the mouth with her other hand, put him down, and then calmly looked us over. "I trust, children," she said, "that from now on, you will remember Rule One." We sure did! When we didn't, our scalps regretted our forgetfullness.

She then called the roll. Rule Two was that the moment she said your name, you had to be out from behind your desk, stand stiffly erect beside it and say "Present, Miss Polson." Because those desks were sometimes too small for some of us bigger boys to extricate ourselves in time, we waited hair-trigger to jump out in a hurry. Miss Polson prowled about the room during roll call, occasionally examining us if we looked unkempt. "You're neck is dirty, young man. Go to the washroom!" she'd say. Or she'd look at our hands to see if they were clean. One time she kept Fisheye in at recess and combed his hair so hard he almost died. In calling the roll, Miss Polson always used our full names but she never was able to get Fisheye's right. She called him "Thissate" although it really was supposed to be pronounced Tisseye, which is where his nickname came from. French doesn't have any *th* and the final *t's* are omitted, but Miss Polson said it the way it was spelled - Thissate. She also had trouble on some of the Finn names, but no one argued with P. P. Polson. We just learned our new names.

Next, we pledged the oath of allegiance to the flag and not just by moving our lips either, as Lily Tomplin discovered to her sorrow. Miss Polson didn't lift her up by the hair; she merely cocked her second finger against the thumb and snapped it against Lily's ear. Although more than sixty years have passed, my own ears still tingle with the remembering.

In the morning sessions we had Grammar and Mathematics, then all too short recess of fifteen minutes, then History. Our afternoon classes were in Geography, Literature and Palmer Writing. No recess in the afternoon. The ones I hated most were Grammar and Palmer Writing. Miss Polson punished us not only for breaking her rules but also for not knowing our stuff. I remember one miserable experience up at the blackboard in front of the class when I had to diagram and phrase the sentence "*Only* Cully tried to fool Miss Polson and he *only* tried once." That word "only" was my undoing. Maybe the first *only* could be stretched enough to call it an adjective because it modified my name, a noun, but the second *only* came before "tried," a verb. How could that damned word be both an adjective and an adverb? My skull learned that it could when Miss Polson's hard knuckles impressed the fact upon it.

But the Palmer Writing was the worst. Gad, how I hated making those interminable ovals and push-pulls and never getting them right. No, that's not quite true. Once I made three perfect ovals in a row but when I tried to put the up and down push-pulls in them, I overfilled the quill of my pen in the inkwell and plastered a huge glob of ink on the last one. Miss Polson did her best to motivate me but getting hit on the wrists with her ruler didn't help even though she did it five times before finally giving up on me.

At that, I was luckier than many of the other boys probably because I did well in the other subjects. Even so, I never once got a hundred on any report card. Miss Polson was a perfectionist and a hard grader. The best I ever got was a ninety-nine in history. Not in deportment! Though I tried to stay out of trouble, I never managed it. There were many opportunities.

Most of them came when Miss Polson had to go to the bathroom. They said she had weak kidneys - or maybe they were too strong. Anyway, two or three times each morning and afternoon she'd leave us alone in the classroom for a few minutes. (That's why, behind her back, we called her P. P. It wasn't because her full name was Paula Penelope Polson.) Sometimes we could see her getting restless, crossing and uncrossing her legs under her desk, and then she'd say, "Continue, children!" and make a dash for it. We rarely continued.

All hell would break loose. That's when the snakes or toads appeared to put the girls screaming atop their seats, Or the mice. Or Mullu eating a big worm. That's when the spitballs flew. That's when the snuff got put in the water cooler. That's when we hid her dreaded ruler or greased the end of her chalk so it wouldn't write. That's when someone put the egg in her snowboots.

Someone always kept an eye on that doorknob though, and when he saw it turn he'd say "Pssst!" and we'd be very good boys and girls studying hard again at our desks when P. P. returned, trying our utmost to keep from laughing. We had to be pretty careful, too, that P. P. wasn't faking it. Pipu Salmi sure got caught right in the act of putting a tack on her chair when she went out and came right back. For a long time, too, we couldn't figure out how she always was able to pick out the kid doing the devilment and punish him good until we found that she'd got Charley Olafson, our town marshall and school janitor, to bore a little peephole in the door.

Of course, we did some monkey business too even when she was right in the room but looking the other way. One favorite trick was to get a piece of rubber band, put it on the end of a pencil, pull it back and let fly. Gee, that sure hurt when you got it in the back of the neck. Our favorite target for rubber banding was Eva Thomas who had once tattled on us. She'd always yelp good. Even though Eva never tattled again after we soaked her pigtails in the inkwell, we never quite forgave her that one time. No tattling was *our* Rule One.

Not all of P. P.'s punishments were physical. She had a sarcastic tongue that could scrape the hide off our dirty little psyches. She also believed in making her punishment fit our crime. Any paper that contained even one spelling error had to be rewritten before you went home that night no matter how long you had to stay after school. Any grammatical mistake you happened to make in an oral recitation she wrote on the blackboard with your name beside it, and you had to write it correctly one hundred times, no matter how many recesses it took.

I don't know how P. P. did it, but she also had an uncanny ability to guess who'd done the mischief while she was in the bathroom. Once, when Untu had plastered a nice juicy spitball on the ceiling over her head by using a ruler as a catapult, and we waited for it to dry and fall down, she identified him immediately, picked him up by the ears, and shook him hard. Perhaps it was because he looked more innocent than the rest of us. That time, P. P. had to lift him by his ears instead of his hair because all of us boys had gotten our heads shaved. Shaved, not crew cut. I remember how unhappy my mother was when she saw me come home from the barber's, but I wasn't going to be the only boy with hair to pull out.

Speaking of spitballs, I got caught myself once because I wanted a supply ready when she left the room. I thought I was safe because I was chewing the paper pretty slyly and only when she wasn't looking. Later I figured out how she did it. P. P. really didn't have eyes in the back of her head. As she cleaned her glasses by covering one of them, it acted like a mirror. Anyway, she caught me, and that afternoon I had to stay after school and make spitballs until my tongue was hanging out, my mouth was so dry.

Yet there were times when P. P. did show a little mercy. When Untu, in geography class, said that capital was the turkey of Constantinople and we laughed, she punished us not him. She knew Untu always got his words mixed up and that only Finnish was spoken in his home. Another time, when Felix Poulet mispronounced some easy words, she didn't make him carry the baby nursing bottle all day like she did with others of us because his folks spoke French.

Much as we hated the old bugger, we had to admit that we sure learned a lot in that grade. I still remember how the Chinese made silk and that the British burned Buffalo in the War of 1812. I can still recite long passages from Shakespeare's Macbeth. To wit:

"Round about the cauldron go,
In the poisoned entrails throw.
Toad, that under cold stone,
Days and nights hast thirty-one.
Sweltered Venom sleeping got,
Boiled thou first in charmed pot.
Double, double, toil and trouble,
Burning fire and cauldron bubble."

Yes, Miss Polson sure made those witches of Endor come alive. She was one! Always too, we had to understand what we were reading because she checked up by having us paraphrase in our own words. Woe if we couldn't! P. P. also was a great one for mental multiplication. It disciplined our minds, she said, and by the end of that year we were doing three place numbers in our heads - or getting our tails disciplined. As you can imagine, our parents were much impressed. They agreed with old Blue Balls, our superintendent, that P. P. Polson sure knew how to teach.

Very rarely did she ever praise any one of us and when she did, you felt as though you'd been awarded the Congressional Medal of Honor or something. Just hearing her say, "Well done" was a real event. I suppose I remember her telling me once that I was a good thinker because the kids for days afterwards kept mimicking her, "Cully, you're a good stinker!" I got a bloody nose in a fight about that teasing.

I also remember how the days dragged that spring and how hard it was to sit still when the birds were singing outside the open window and the trout were waiting for me down in Beaver Dam Creek. At the end of each school day, we kids almost went crazy. We'd run around in circles, like young colts in their first pasture. We'd holler and scream all the way home and fight each other like maniacs.

Finally, at long last, our ordeal year with Miss Polson was almost over. We had a school picnic and then the next day returned for a brief hour to clean out our desks. On the playground before the bell rang, all of us were reciting, not Shakespeare but "Goodbye, P. P., Goodbye school! Goodbye, P. P. Damned old fool."

After calling the roll and hearing us pledge allegiance to the flag one last time, she made a little speech. "Children, (how we hated that term!), it has been my pleasure to have had you as my pupils for many months. I trust that you have profited! You will be glad to know that I have sought and been granted permission from our superintendent, Mr. Donegal, to be your next year's teacher too."

Geez! No fair!

Cully Gage, author of *Heads and Tales*, a third Northwoods Reader.

Susan Krill, daughter of Cully Gage, is the illustrator of *Heads and Tales.*

TIOGA
METHODIST
CHURCH
SERVICES
SUNDAY
BIBLE STUDY
WEDNESDAY
LAHAN'S
TORE